Strange and Wonderful Things

A Collection of Ghost Stories
with Special Appearances
by Witches and Other Bizarre Creatures

Thomas L. Freese

PublishAmerica
Baltimore

ISBN: 1-60563-974-5
PUBLISHED BY PUBLISHAMERICA, LLLP
www.publishamerica.com
Baltimore

Printed in the United States of America

Table of Contents

The Witch's Rake

I have seen people remember a promise made for a long time and I know that a wish or prayer can last for decades, waiting for the right time to come alive. We never forget a kindness done to us. How much more so do we wish to repay someone who saved the life of those who we love?

Mr. Solomon was one of the last remaining World War II veterans in town. His wife was dead for 10 years and he had little to do on most days except take care of his large yard. He had a large brick colonial style house, surrounded by a four acre lot with many trees. There were old oaks, holly, maple and a few willow trees. He was usually outside by 8am, sweeping the stone pathway, picking up fallen sticks or raking leaves. He was tall with a full head of white hair. And when he worked near the front iron gate or fence running along Main Street, the children talked with him. Sometimes he carried mints or hard candy in his pockets for them. He liked to rake the leaves in numerous little piles to easily scoop them into a bag lined trash can. He worked in a neat manner also picking up sticks, breaking them into uniform foot-long pieces. The holly wood, where broken, showed white inside. He fancied they looked like teeth. And so it is with many retirees as they putter about their house and yard with little else for amusement.

Mr. Solomon was a paratrooper and his unit saw action in the invasions in both Italy and France—D-Day. He was stationed in England before D-Day with the 101st Airborne. Early on June 6th his unit was dropped almost 20 miles from the target zone and in the darkness, he found some British paratroopers. In their predawn battle, Mr. Solomon saved the life of one of the British soldiers. They later exchanged names and kept in touch, writing a few letters as they battled across Europe. That soldier, Ian Dawson, didn't make it through the war and his widow wrote him until the 1950's. She wrote again in early 1969, inviting Mr. and Mrs. Solomon to visit her in Somerset. She reasoned in her letter that many war veterans would be traveling that spring for the 25 year anniversary of D-Day.

The Solomon's decided to travel to France and England that June and it was a good trip for both of them. Mr. Solomon visited the graves of his comrades and Mrs. Solomon better understood the sacrifice the Allied soldiers made. After Normandy, they traveled by boat to Britain and found themselves in Mrs. Dawson's country cottage in Priston, in Somerset. They were her guests for several days, enjoying teas and scones, while Mrs. Dawson talked about her late husband. No one mentioned again that Mr. Solomon saved him. But the night before they left, Mr. Solomon had an interesting chat with Mrs. Dawson. While Mrs. Solomon showered, Mrs. Dawson took his hand and walked him outside to the tool shed.

"Edward" she called him by his first name, "I want to tell you about something that happened in early 1945."

He looked bewildered and glanced around the tool shed. There were garden tools and hanging bunches of herbs and all were lit by the late spring sunset, glowing yellow.

"On the same day that my husband was reported killed in action, the date I learned later, I believe he came to me and gave me a message. I was sleeping a restless sleep and awoke to see a figure at the foot of my bed. The figure was dark against the bright moonlight but I knew it was Ian and I knew he had been killed. I slowly sat up in bed and waited to see if he would speak. I held my breath to see what my husband's spirit would want me to know.

"He said he loved me and not to worry about how he

died, that it didn't matter. He said he had to go but he added one last message. He told me to take care of you, Edward. He told me, 'You know how to do that.'"

Mr. Solomon felt a bit uncomfortable with Mrs. Dawson so close in this small tool shed. What did the message mean and how did she mean to take care of him? She continued.

"You see, Edward, my people have lived on this land for many generations. We have wisdom of life and the land and we understand how to protect and please those who show friendship and loyalty. I shan't tell you more but I brought you out here to give you something."

Mrs. Dawson reached toward the shed wall to take down a rake. She held it and looked only at the rake while speaking to him.

"One of my family many years ago made this rake, Edward. It is a special tool, made with loving hands. The handle is made of holly, known to the Celts as a good wood for spear shafts, so that signifies strength in battle. The rakes themselves are made of yew. You see, Edward, we plant yew in churchyards and it is a special wood that never dies and is reborn by sending new tree shoots out from the decayed old trunk. If something made of wood is loved and respected, then the tree spirits never leave that wooden thing. I want you to have and keep this rake. Ian used it and I know he would like you to keep it."

She then looked up at Edward, searching his eyes for a reaction. He was surprised at his own acceptance, having traveled across the Atlantic to receive an antique garden rake, unfazed and suspending doubt that Mrs. Dawson was...a witch?

"Thank you very much, Mrs. Dawson. I know this means a lot to you to give me something from your family and that Ian used." Mrs. Dawson smiled, as Mrs. Solomon called from the back porch, looking for the two.

Then Mrs. Dawson added, "I think you might want to keep the rake on your front porch and not locked up in your garage."

Mr. Solomon carried the rake back and showed it to his wife. She thought it odd and quaint that Mrs. Dawson gave him the rake but she figured that she was still a grieving widow and allowed her that eccentric expression of friendship. After they returned to Kentucky, Mr. Solomon kept that rake handy and often used it to rake the leaves. But it wasn't until after his wife passed away, years later, that he began to notice unusual things about the rake.

Mr. Solomon had a rather obnoxious neighbor, on his south side, for three years. The man was afraid of burglars and kept several German shepherds in his yard. But he also had a fence with numerous holes and his dogs wandered over to Mr. Solomon's yard. Edward was captured in the Battle of the Bulge by the Germans and due to some circumstances while a prisoner, he was afraid of German shepherd dogs. One summer day, Mr. Solomon walked briskly out his front walk to get the morning newspaper. He hadn't noticed his neighbor's male, black shepherd, behind the maple tree. The dog bared his teeth and then charged. Mr. Solomon barely made it back to the front door in time to pull open the screen door and race inside. His heart raced for some 30 minutes afterward. He sat down on the sofa to calm down and try and let the war flashback fade away. While Mr. Solomon sat down, he was unaware that the rake flew off the porch and headed handle-first toward the German shepherd. The dog must have seen more than just a rake, as he let out a yelp, ears back, tail between his legs and dashed toward the fence. The dog managed to dive through the fence hole but not before the animated rake gave him a sound wallop on his flank. Mr. Solomon heard the dog cry out and later wondered why he no longer had unwelcome canine visitors in his yard.

One Halloween, Mr. Solomon entertained children dressed as ghosts and ghouls. The rake of course was there on the front porch. Some teenagers approached his house. None of them wore costumes and they demanded, in rough tones, candy. He reluctantly gave them some chocolates but when he closed the door, he was afraid they might vandalize his house or stay for more mischief. They huddled a few feet away from the front door as Mr. Solomon slowly lifted a window blind to see what they intended to do. There was an orange glowing light that came from the porch. The teenagers heard a weird sound coming from the porch. It was the rake. They thought it was Mr. Solomon playing a spooky record to scare them. So they reached into their brown paper bags, where they hid rocks and eggs, determined to have their mean entertainment. But both Mr. Solomon and the teenagers were shocked as the rake let out a screeching sound. Although all Edward saw was a garden rake, flying about on its own, chasing away the boys, he did have a feeling from their terrorized faces that they saw something much more threatening.

Mr. Solomon walked outside one mid-October morning to rake leaves. He expected some help from two sisters, Mary and Ann Cavallo. He paid them for their yard work. They were mischievous but helped him rake leaves the previous year. They seemed overly curious about his collectibles in his living room when he invited them after raking leaves to offer them milk and cookies. This year, each time they visited, they asked to stay inside a while. They particularly liked Mrs. Solomon's jewelry collection, asking to try on necklaces and earrings. The girls were in sixth and fifth grades. Mary was older, with jet black hair and dark eyes, and Ann had lighter, longer hair and was thin.

Mr. Solomon didn't realize it at the time but with each visit the girls stole things. Sometimes it was money and other times it was jewelry or one of Mrs. Solomon's pretty things. Each time they came to work and then visited inside afterwards, the rake rattled when they passed through the front door. Worse than the thievery, the girls took photographs from Mr. Solomon's album. They took old pictures of his time in the war, marriage and early family years. And when they looked at the pictures, back at their house, they burned them! But one photo just didn't seem to take a match and never burned. That was the service photo of Ian Dawson.

The girls showed up late. It was nearly noon when Mr. Solomon showed them to the back yard to help break sticks. He worked nearby, taking leaves out of the small goldfish pond. The girls gossiped about their friends and laughed at how they fooled their parents, staying out late to drink and run around town. Mr.

Solomon slowly walked over to them and thanked them for helping.

He said, "You know girls, I couldn't help but hearing you all talking. You know, about your friends and family, I just have to say, you might want to be careful and be more respectful of others. I've seen that bad people can end up in a very different place than good people."

The girls acted innocently, feigning ignorance of the meaning of his warning. He began to know that something was amiss with these two and that things went missing in his house.

Mary asked, in a sweet but deceiving, flirty voice, "Mr. Solomon, could we come in your house and take a break?"

"Yeah, Mr. Solomon," Ann added, "We love to look at your old time stuff." Mary flashed her sister a warning look but smiled quickly at Mr. Solomon.

"Okay girls, we can pick up all the piles of leaves tomorrow, if you want to come back."

They visited again inside for milk and cookies and the girls thrilled to look at his coin collection. When they left by the front porch, Mary was carrying an extra house key to his house in her jeans. The rake seemed to fall forward toward Mary. The handle smacked her upper thigh—right where she put his house key. Mr. Solomon apologized and told them that the wind must have pushed the rake over.

It was windy, there were storms coming that night. The girls left and Mr. Solomon went inside to start fixing dinner. After dinner he read a favorite book and fell asleep on the couch.

It was after midnight, when the Cavallo girls walked back from a friend's house. They had in mind to use the house key to Mr. Solomon's house that night, to go inside and steal some real goodies. But as they talked in hushed voices walking down Main Street, the witch's rake came alive. It flew around the large yard, raking all the little piles of leaves into one huge pile. And it raked together a pile of holly sticks, putting those into the big leaf pile.

The girls quietly opened the front gate. They were excited about being bad and the wind seemed to push them off the walkway toward the pile of leaves.

"Cool, check out this huge pile of leaves!" Ann was wide-eyed with delight.

"Come on let's jump in it before we go inside! Ann grabbed her older sister's hand, pulling her toward the dark tangle of oak leaves.

"Why don't we play after we steal his stuff?" Mary asked.

But her younger sister just giggled and said, "We have plenty of time, come on!"

So the two girls ran the remaining twenty feet and still holding hands jumped into the air above the leaf pile. The pile then opened wide, very wide, with a dark and evil space below. All the holly sticks lined the huge open mouth, showing white and sharp. And at the moment the shocked and surprised girls knew what was going to happen to them, they realized that indeed bad people end up in a very different place than good people.

The Healing Child

"Sticks and stones will break my bones but lies will never hurt me" is an old proverb which reminds us that words cannot harm us. When grief grips our heart, perhaps words alone won't bring healing but rather time and love acting through simple messages—in this story—sticks and stones.

"Grandpa, read me a story!"

"No not tonight. It's too late." Grandpa looked into his granddaughter's eyes and knew that excuse wouldn't do.

"John, you know it's her regular bedtime."

Grandma Catherine finished tucking in her eight year old, favorite and only granddaughter.

John sighed and turned to her to say, "But I've been doing paperwork all day and my eyes are tired." Grandma Catherine raised one eyebrow and he looked up and sighed in frustration.

"I've got to finish cooking for tomorrow, John. I'm sure you'll think of something."

Grandpa John turned back to look at Katy—sweet and innocent and smiling like an angel. *I'm so tired of reading the same old storybooks,* he thought. *But maybe...I can tell a story.*

"Okay, here's the deal, Katy. Grandpa has very tired eyes and I won't be reading you a story tonight"—Katy looked shocked—"but I can tell you a story."

"What kind of story are you going to tell me—one about dragons and princesses and evil witches? Katy sat up quickly, wondering if Grandpa John really was a storyteller like her Dad once said.

"No Katy, nothing like that at all."

"Oh...then what is the story about?" Katy looked puzzled. John wondered if he should tell this tale about her father.

"Well," he started slowly, "it is a story about your Daddy, about how he became a doctor and works with children."

Katy looked indignantly at Grandpa John and said, "I know the grown up word for what my Daddy does. He is a pediatrician!"

"Yes, of course, Katy. You're right. He's a pediatrician—now. But years ago, he was not so sure about what he wanted to do in life. In fact, he was an unhappy young man."

With a frowning face, Katy asked, "What do you mean Grandpa?"

Grandpa John thought carefully for a moment and then continued.

"Well, Katy, sometimes when people are young, they don't know exactly what they want to do or be in life and it can take a while to figure that out. Let me tell the story from the beginning. Since we're not looking at a picture book together, let me turn off the ceiling light. You can lie back and let the pictures of the story flow through your mind."

Grandpa John got up from the bed and walked over

to flip the wall switch. Katy pulled her tiger and purple unicorn stuffed animals close to her as she lay down on her side and watched Grandpa. He hesitated for a moment, looking toward the kitchen where his wife opened the oven door.

Grandpa John walked back and pulled a bedside chair across the fuzzy blue carpet, took off his shoes and set his feet up on Katy's bed. She reached over to tickle his faded blue socks and they both laughed.

"I love you Grandpa." Katy said and Grandpa's eyes quickly watered. He leaned over to hug her.

"I love you too, Katybug."

"Grandpa..." said Katy, stretching out his name in protest, as she tilted her head and plopped back down on her pillow. "Tell the story now."

"Okay," he said.

"Quite some time ago, your Dad was in high school. He was smart but a lot of times it seemed he didn't really want to study. That got worse by the time he got into college and he often skipped classes. By his second year, it was obvious to everyone that he had to drop out. That's when came back here to our farm. The college counselor said that he was having problems because he was depressed."

Katy asked, "You mean he was sad?"

"Yes Katy, the counselor thought he was very sad about something. We weren't sure exactly what he was so sad about although later we found out it was because of his friend."

"What happened to his friend?" Katy said, hesitating, as if she might not really want to know.

"Robert...err, your Dad, had a friend...Well, let's see, I think your daddy was about your age when it happened. Your Dad's friend was a few years younger than you. They were best buddies since they could walk. Brian came over every day. He thought the world of your daddy. They played sports, board games, went walking...well, they just about did everything together. Sometimes Brian stayed for dinner and his Father had to come over and remind him to come back to their home to sleep for the night!"

Grandpa just stopped talking.

"What happened next, Grandpa?" Grandpa John picked up one of Katy's stuffed animals that fell on the floor. It was a floppy-eared brown dog. He pushed back the dog's hair from his eyes as if petting a real dog.

"Grandpa—what happened?!" Katy's eyebrows furrowed together and Grandpa John continued.

"Brian had a dog that ran everywhere, sometimes out in the street. Your Dad and Brian were playing when Brian chased his dog past some parked cars but a man driving a truck didn't see Brian. Brian was very hurt and they took him away to the hospital. Your Daddy was shocked and very sad. Brian died in the hospital later that day."

It was very quiet and Katy seemed to be thinking.

She said, "Grandpa, that's so sad..." Grandpa John heard a soft noise behind him and turned in his chair to see Grandma Catherine standing in the open doorway.

"John..." she started to say and he interrupted quickly "You know that the rest of the story is better and ends happy."

She looked worried and walked over to them both.

She looked at Katy and said, "Just remember that God loves all of us and his angels protect us no matter what happens, okay?"

"Okay" smiled Katy as Grandma hugged her and then left, adding, "We're going shopping tomorrow, just us girls."

"I know Grandma." Then Katy whispered, "Finish the story, Grandpa!"

Grandpa John looked thoughtfully at Katy and then continued.

"Your Dad really didn't want to do much at all when he came back. He slept a lot and we tried to get him to see another counselor but he wouldn't go. He only played his guitar and took walks. We tried to talk to him about making plans for work or going back to college. But he said that it just didn't matter.

"Since we have 300 acres here, there are lots of places to go hiking. You know that since we've taken you around some places on the farm. But your Daddy liked to go to the farther places to be alone. We were a little worried about him and sometimes he hiked for hours and hours, even missing lunch or dinner. Though we worried when he came back after dark, he always seemed in a better mood after hiking. He went in any weather—sunny, cloudy, windy, snowy and rainy—he just needed to get outside and be with the trees, rocks and birds.

"I couldn't help but following him one time. It was after he even stopped playing guitar and Grandma and I were so worried for him. I waited to see which way he headed out from our house. I was pretty sure he was walking toward the creek with the crumbly white sandstone. Since it was a little muddy, I followed his shallow footprints in the soft low grass. It was November and I could see my breath. I came over the rise above the creek and I saw him down in the creek bed, squatting down, playing with a stick in the sand. He seemed happy and at peace, like a child.

"I backed away from the hill's edge, so he wouldn't hear me and walked back to our house, wondering what it meant. I remember a friend, who is a psychiatrist, saying that Robert might be 'regressing'. He explained that sometimes grownups need to act like a child again to feel better. I just hoped that your Daddy would be happy again.

"Now I want to tell you the rest of the story, Katybug. This part of the story is what your Dad told me just a few years ago."

Katy looked up at her Grandfather's eyes and asked, "Is Daddy still sad about Brian?"

"No Katy, and maybe when you hear the rest of the story, you will understand."

"Your Dad said that he felt angry and sad back then. He wasn't really thinking about Brian. He was mostly just frustrated with himself, that he wasn't able to decide about what he thought might be important. He said his walks were like hiking into his own soul, to find out what was the matter. He walked everyday and he liked to look around and observe the trees, find feathers or special rocks. I remember he brought some home and set them on the patio table.

"One day, Robert walked down the path along the old pasture. It's now dotted with cedars. He couldn't help but almost stumble on a set of rocks, set right on the path, in the shape of an arrow. Someone put a very clear sign to go in the direction the arrow pointed. The arrow was made up of small gray field stones. There was a straight line of rocks and two short diagonal lines at the arrow's tip. He was puzzled and wondered if I set those out for him. He couldn't think of anyone else since your Grandmother doesn't hike out there and there aren't any neighbors that come on our property. But he followed the arrow, headed north on the path which led to the end of the pasture into the woods. There he found another, smaller rock arrow and this he followed another three hundred feet. The path then veered right, where he would usually walk but instead, a third rock arrow bent to the left and he followed it through thickening brush until it stopped at a cliff face. Something he would not notice in summer, when the leaves of brush and trees cover the rocky cliff, was there glittering in the winter sun. It was a large grouping of quartz crystals. Your Dad said he stood there for some time and then he smiled. He realized that *someone* planned this pleasant surprise for only his discovery.

"Although he suspected that I set out the rock arrows, he kept quiet for weeks, waiting to see if he could catch me. For he continued to find more stones or sticks, set outside and they always led him to some special feature of the land or some natural thing he would not himself notice. After a while, he said, the rocks reduced to simply two or three stones and he quickly adjusted to this truncated code. A stick, he said, indicated direction by which of the sticks' ends were thinner and so it was with a single rock. The sticks and stones led your Dad to simple, little things, like a pretty blue jay feather, or a bird's nest.

"The odd thing was, your Dad said, whenever he returned from the indicated destination, the rock or stick signs disappeared. That really made him wonder, for he thought if Grandpa put out the stones, Grandpa wouldn't be quiet enough to put them away without him hearing me. And he said the sign stones weren't just kicked or scattered away off the path— they were carefully set back to wherever they were taken. It was a mystery, and it kept your Father engaged in life and it began to lift his depression. He felt that someone, perhaps a child, was playing with him. He realized that he didn't always have to look down for their signs. Once he stopped at favorite spot, where a spring bubbles out of the rocky ground above the mossy creek. He saw, just at the height of his eyes, a carefully crafted willow circle, dangling on a branch. Another time, when he stopped again at the creek with the white sandstone, he looked into a pool of water and saw, set on the creek's pebbled bottom, a pattern of old broken glass pieces, colored in cobalt blues, greens and lavender. The glass pieces meandered around in spirals and curves.

"Your Dad said the messages continued all winter. He said, on Valentine's Day, he followed some stick arrows past the big river into the flood plain. There he found a heart shaped group of stones. When he looked closely, inside the heart, he found five small bunny rabbits cautiously eyeing him from under the loose grass. He backed up and sat down on a fallen log. That's when he knew that I couldn't have set up the stones, since he was past that way two days before and he had not seen the stones. And he knew that I was out of town all week.

"Your Daddy said that as the spring came, with more sunlight and happy birds and animals, he began to feel better. He wasn't as sad and angry as before. He started to realize that it didn't matter if he dropped out of college. He talked more to us and his appetite returned.

"Then one spring night we had a terrible thunderstorm. After Robert helped me clear fallen branches from the telephone lines, he asked to go for a walk. He said he felt the air was much different, something had changed, something had left—the air was fresh and clear and he had to get out and enjoy it. He walked for hours, heading back toward the hills and boulders. He saw no signs, but rather followed an urge to go to the very edge of our land, where the hills lead to the high land of our neighbors."

Grandpa John stopped and looked at Katy. Her eyes drooped and her breathing had become more slow and shallow.

"Go on, Grandpa" she drowsily said but it was obvious that she would soon fall asleep. Grandpa John smiled and touched a lock of blond hair on her forehead.

"Okay, honey."

"Your Daddy didn't see any sticks or stones that day, pointing the way. Somehow he knew he had to find something that day, something on his own. He walked up to a line of tumbled down rocks, large rocks and continued westward. Then he saw that a large old pine tree was struck by lightning. As he got closer, he smelled and then saw the smoldering base of the tree, fully blasted in half. The larger tree trunk section fell south, away from the hills. And there, between the tree base and the boulder behind was something strange. At first, he didn't recognize the smooth dark rock, back where dark pine branches had fallen for decades."

Katy was sleeping. She looked so pretty and peaceful but Grandpa John continued.

"Your Daddy realized that it was a gravestone. He reached over the smoky pine tree to sweep away branches and pine needles. It was a tall, narrow black slate gravestone. Despite the age, the letters and numbers carefully chiseled so long ago were readable. They said, *here lies our beloved son, Jonas Pruitt, born 1797 died 1802.* Your Daddy stood there for some time, he said, before he started crying. He said he sobbed like a little child, falling over to curl up on the soft orange pine needles. When he finally stopped crying, he felt a great pain drained out of his heart. He thought very much of Brian but it was another child entirely who healed his grief."

Of course, Katy was sleeping and Grandpa John sat and watched her for a few minutes. He set the stuffed dog by her side, turned out the light at the bedside and walked out of the room.

"Sweet dreams, Katybug."

Perfect Work Record

I know some children who brag about their perfect school attendance and other folks, adults, who never missed a day of work. But I remember skipping school as an 8ᵗʰ grader. We didn't do anything extraordinary or really even naughty. But it did open my eyes, just a little, to see that even good habits have a limit and on certain work days, it might be better to stay home.

Andrea Anderson was a model employee. She drove a bus for the Bullitt County schools and never missed a day despite having worked for 37 years. While school board members, principals and even teachers, came and went, Mrs. Andy was as steady as the morning sun, as regular as flowing river water and as dependable as the Lord's good grace. She kept the bus in her own yard and got up at 5am every school day to begin her morning ritual.

Mrs. Andy started each work day by getting dressed, fixing bacon and eggs for her husband then herself and drinking coffee while listening to the latest weather report. Mrs. Andy then saw her husband off to work. He left to drive south to the interstate. Afterwards she drove north to start her route of picking up 28 to 30 elementary age students.

It was all so very familiar and automatic. She could probably compose a symphony or solve mathematical formulas in her mind while she went the decades-old route. She first drove downhill along her gravel driveway, right on 1442 and over the long, old concrete bridge that spanned two sections of the Salt River. Then Mrs. Andy picked up kids in neighborhoods off Bardstown Road and Stringer Lane before dropping them off at Mt. Washington Elementary School.

She saw all kinds of weather from floods to icy streets to heavy snowfalls and downed trees. In 1974, she managed to safely return all her children to their homes before a tornado swept away children from a schoolyard in adjacent Meade County. Mrs. Andy could put chains on all the bus tires in ten minutes and she even knew a few tricks for getting a reluctant engine started on a cold winter morning. She felt good about her work record. She wasn't proud but she knew that those kids depended on her. She considered their convenience before her safety. Some folks suggested that she should drive the long way around to the newer bridge over the Salt River but she figured that would likely put the kids in too late.

One spring not long ago, Kentucky had extraordinary rains each month from March through May. And it was on the morning of Friday, May 13, that Andrea Anderson got up at 5am to begin another day...

"Don't we have any more strawberry jam?" Mr. Anderson complained. He scrunched over his plate of scrambled eggs and thick bacon.

"Shh—I'm trying to hear the weather report!" Mrs. Andy turned the volume higher as the announcer spoke quickly:

"...Record rainfall amounts forecast, from five to eight inches of rain have fallen overnight and more expected immediately. Local flooding likely with road ponding reported on I-65 since overnight."

"Don't count on taking 1442" Mr. Anderson chimed in, "you know the water can easily rise up to the top of that old bridge."

Mrs. Andy threw him a worried look as he walked off to brush his teeth. She finished dressing and looked out the bedroom window to see sheets of rain falling. She kissed Mr. Anderson goodbye and he left their 1949 bungalow to drive his red Ford truck away into the gloom. She had to admit, the dark feeling was more than the weather outside working at her insides. The night before when she was doing the Courier crossword puzzle, she was stuck on an intersecting pair of words at 29 down and 14 across. Just before falling asleep she solved first one and then the other word. The words were inundation and specter.

Mrs. Andy grabbed her yellow rain jacket and slipped on her boots. It was 6:15am. While the bus warmed up she checked on the school radio but was unable to reach them. Since there were some hills on her side of the county, reception was poor until she got closer to open land at the Salt River. She released the brake and the bus, previously parked to point downhill, rolled along past blooming redbud and dog wood trees. As she turned right on 1442, she could see the creek across Johnson's farm was swollen and moving fast with debris of logs and trash.

She realized she could have waited until maybe 6:45 to call the school office before leaving but she figured that the kids she picked up lived on higher ground. So even if school opened on a delayed schedule or if it was cancelled, she would find out by the time she picked up the Maloney twins, first on her route, off Bardstown Road. Her bus shifted automatically as she followed the winding road down to the Salt River valley. She knew that the river would be up, high and flooding but she wasn't prepared to see, as she turned the final curve, the extent of the width and violence of the muddy brown water.

She saw water up everywhere and the water was flooding over parts of the bridge. As she drove up, she felt a chill and almost put the bus in reverse. She could see that the middle section had maybe four inches of water flowing through the concrete side railing. But beyond that section of about fifty feet, the north side of the bridge was clear. She put her foot to the accelerator with a spunky determination and figured that a few inches of water wouldn't keep her from her duty.

But the real danger lay underneath, as the bridge pilings were pummeled all night by the rushing power of water pushing submerged logs into the bridge. The structure was going to give and it was an unfortunate thing that it gave way precisely as Mrs. Andy reached the middle section.

She screamed as she realized that the water was taking a hold of the rear of the bus and as she and the bus were spun around ninety degrees in a second, the whole south bridge section disappeared into the turbulent, dark waters. The bus hung suspended for about five seconds before it slipped into the water. And in those few seconds, Andrea Anderson sat with a dazed look, still strapped in her seat and said a prayer. It wasn't exactly a prayer for her well being but she did ask for divine help nevertheless.

At 6:41am, the Maloney twins looked out their living room window and shouted, "Mom, the bus is here!"

They ran out in the driving rain and Mrs. Andy opened the hinged doors. They both exclaimed about the heavy rain as they went past their faithful bus driver but she didn't talk. Mrs. Andy clutched the wheel with icy hands and a large pool of water was at her feet.

Some people said they saw the bus that morning that picked up their children while others did not. But the bus did its full run and all the kids who were ready to be picked up that day made it to school. Mrs. Hite watched her son Malcolm run to the bus but for some reason, the bus seemed shrouded in a fog or mist. And all the children who rode that morning commented that Mrs. Andy looked so pale. They said she wasn't smiling. Maybe she was very worried about making it to school. At Mt. Washington Elementary, Bus Number 1 opened its doors and the children walked past the cold figure and distant eyes of Mrs. Andy. She kept her perfect work record for one more bus run.

Dust Bunnies

One of the constant chores of domestic life from our ancestors clearing out the cave clutter to modern vacuuming robots is our reluctant duty to straighten, dust and clean our home and possessions. Although we prefer to do other chores or to simply avoid the work altogether, cobwebs and other messes can build up and literally trip us. And there may be deeper wisdom in the words 'Cleanliness is next to Godliness' than we realize. Perhaps danger lurks in messiness and dirt.

Alfred P. Skinner was old school. He lived at the edge of town and rarely came into be seen by normal folks. He was a grown-up only child now 61 years old. He saved money in every conceivable way, growing his own food, hunting and even raising rabbits for food. His home was his parent's home, the house where he grew up and their antiquated and dusty furniture still stood in the same spots, unmoved for decades. There were layers of clutter and dirt, old newspapers, magazines and just junk, everywhere. Alfred himself had a cluttered face, often dirty, sweaty and with hairy gray beard and thinned black and gray hair on top.

He had one aging Aunt Susan, who felt duty-bound

to come once a month and clean her sister's old home and check on Alfred. She usually drove up his overgrown gravel driveway on the first Saturday of the month. On this first Saturday of March, with large but sparse snowflakes falling, Susan drove her old brown Buick up his drive. She walked past the huge bushes in front, noticing that the snow, melted on the ground and brick, was neatly caught in the cobwebs amongst the bushes. She knew to simply walk in the front door, as Alfred was almost always out back, killing some rabbits for his own dinner or for sale, or working his large garden. She didn't look out the back windows for him but began to move dirty clothes to the washing machine. Actually, she couldn't see out any of the windows if she tried. They all were spotted with bird droppings, cluttered with spider webs and nearly dark from red dirt blown from the other farms across Washington County.

Earlier outside, Alfred selected ten rabbits to kill and clean. There might be kinder ways to slaughter his rabbits but Alfred used a hatchet to cut off their heads, like one might dispatch a chicken. And he killed them right in front of the other rabbits. He seemed to find a weird satisfaction with the public executions. Neither did he gut and clean the dead rabbits away from the main pens. Whenever he walked up to even feed or water the rabbits, despite their hunger and thirst, the rabbits shrunk away from his cruel hands and heart. Many of his clothes were permanently stained with blood and other parts.

The light flurries flew by Alfred as he threw the innards to the pigs and heaped rabbit fur on a smelly pile. Although the Michelson's, his nearest neighbors, were nearly a full mile south, they often complained of the terrible smell from Alfred's property. It was the smell of accumulated rabbit dung and slaughtered animals. Susan finished five loads of laundry by two o'clock and cooked their lunch with fresh groceries she brought. She called out the back door just as the sunlight leapt from dark western clouds. He set down his knife and barely brushed his bloody hands on his overalls. As he walked away into the house the rabbits moved together to the food and water at the front of their cages.

While Susan waited for him in the kitchen, she reached for the broom, hoping to sweep up some of the large dust bunnies. She saw a movement through the hallway. It was something low and dark, running across the floor.

"Oh my goodness, Alfred—do you have rats?!"

Alfred opened the back door and walked into the kitchen, looking at Susan's panicked face.

"What's the matter now? I threw out all the old magazines you told me to." He looked both defiant and indignant.

"Alfred, I saw something run across the bedroom floor to under your bed." She spoke with some shaking in her voice. "I can clean your house but I can't get rid of rats!"

He shook his head and smiled, "I know I don't have rats. The breeze must've come in and blown things around when I opened the door."

She stirred the soup and looked sideways at him, frowning. He said, "Aren't you going to add some rabbit meat to that soup?"

"Lord, Alfred! You're always eating that horrible

meat! And those poor creatures just live in fear until you chop off their heads! Why don't you trade with Michelson and eat more of the deer meat?"

Alfred sat down and reached for the bread. "I don't have nothing to trade, except garden produce and I preserve all that I have for winter."

Susan carried his soup in a bowl to the table but nearly dropped it, seeing something dark gray again running toward his room.

"Stop me! I can't stay in here to clean your place and cook—there goes another rat!"

Alfred stood up to face her, "Aunt Susan, I don't have any rats in my home. Come on, I'll prove it to you!"

He grabbed her and pulled her along, her black shiny shoes dragging across linoleum floor and then along wooden floorboards.

"Stop it!! I hate rats!" She screamed.

"Oh shut up! Here—I'll look under my bed."

His Aunt Susan quickly moved away, against the bedroom wall, while Alfred bent down to look at the dark mess under his bed. It was hard for him to see, so he swept his calloused hand across the floor, sending smelly socks and papers out from under the bed.

"There's nothing here," he said, "no rats". Susan's face looked very doubtful.

"I know what I saw."

"If there was a rat down here, it would have run out already. I'll sweep under the other side." Alfred walked around the bed, between the bed and his closet. He bent down to kneel and again swept his arm under the bed.

"Ow—darn!" He felt a sharp pain on his finger.

"See I told you!" His Aunt Susan yelled.

Alfred pulled out his bleeding finger and got up to go to the bathroom to wash it. He called backwards to her as he rinsed his finger.

"That wasn't a rat. I think I put some of my wood saws down there a couple of years ago."

Susan reached into the medicine cabinet for some tissue, cutting some to wrap his finger.

"Come on, let's finish lunch. But you need to call an exterminator." Alfred shrugged his shoulders and followed her into the kitchen.

His Aunt Susan left by four PM and Alfred came back in at five to take a work break. When he opened his back door into the house, he thought he caught movement. Something ran around the corner of the hallway. He walked into this bedroom but saw nothing. One of his pairs of leather boots was on the floor by his bed. He didn't notice the chewing marks on the shoes, double teeth marks dug into the heels.

That night, Alfred relaxed in his living room, amidst the clutter. He liked his home and life.

It works for me, doesn't it?

He saw photographs of homes of rich people, all sparse and with lots of space. Those homes didn't look lived-in at all. He turned on the television, slowly falling asleep as the night turned dark. Outside, the temperature dropped and the wind forced the rabbits to huddle together into one dark shape. Inside, another dark shape moved out from under Alfred's bed. It was a bizarre collection of dust, hair, dirt, bits of spider webs and yellowed paper. It was shaped like a large rabbit and it hopped silently around the house, gathering more dust bunnies, more dirt.

Alfred woke up at midnight. He thought he heard a thumping sound but a quick check around the house showed nothing fell.

He said to himself, "Must be the strong wind tonight."

He turned off the TV and went to his bedroom. He undressed in the dark, throwing his bloody overalls into a heap on the floor. When he fell into his bed the old bedsprings squeaked in an odd way. As he drifted to sleep, he fancied the bedsprings squeaked like rabbits when they tried to run away from his hatchet.

Alfred was asleep when a very large dust bunny came out from under his bed. The dark thing quickly bit into his throat, stifled his scream and began a terrible few minutes of butchering. When morning came, there was no Alfred and no more dust bunnies. And in that bedroom, a framed needlepoint above the dresser seemed to be a simple message of what happened. Alfred's mother made those stitches when she was quite young, carefully sewing the Bible message:

"'Vengeance is mine', Romans 12:19."

Whispers

There is no judge, jury or executioner more efficiently cruel than the spread of rumors or lies. Gossiping is a crafty violence that usually keeps the malefactor's hands free from blood and the initiator exempt from responsibility. But in the world of spirit and energy, the rules of the ordinary seldom apply. Your words may indeed come back to haunt you.

Susan Snipe believed in correct, appropriate and even religious behavior. She rigorously applied her standards to her own actions at home, work, social events and church. She went to weekly Mass and gave home-cooked meals to her less fortunate neighbors. She heeded the rules of man and God and never hit or hurt anyone. She raised her three children to be excellent students and was always faithful to her husband Brett. But where no harm was done with temper or outright anger, Susan Snipe slowly, over the years, slipped into one small vice. She was a gossip.

Susan was artful about her comments so as to simply point the way for more investigative types to sniff out and research the true dirt on someone. Once she observed the parish secretary, who was married, out on a date with a man. She knew it was a date because she was far out of Louisville, taking her grandchildren to the water park in Santa Claus, Indiana. She recognized Mary Dotter, despite Mary's big sunglasses, outside the pool and speaking very closely with a handsome man. Mary did not recognize her as she was awash in the wave machine pool with dozens of other swimmers. And it was months later, at the PTO social over snacks when Susan heard a parishioner talk on the theme of straying wives. Susan thoughtfully munched on a cracker.

She said, "It must be so hard for Mrs. Dotter to manage, with her husband gone half the year on business."

There—the thought was planted into the minds of three other women, ladies who often freely conversed in the school and at church. And Susan gave no specific testimony. She merely positioned one conversational thought next to another.

Over the years Susan took pleasure in her small but critical role in assisting with the moral downfall of other members of her community. She felt that she was actually helping divine justice to come to those who were imperfect or inconsistent. Susan passed on "suggestions" on many topics directly related to the failures of her neighbors, such as: health problems, mental disease, fighting families, body handicaps, poor fashion sense, rebellious children, drug use, alcoholic binges, past lives of crime and other indiscretions too numerous to mention. All the while she kept her own life in perfect working order. And for those who suspected that Susan was the originator of the whispering cadre of damaging information, they could find not one secret about Susan and her family to exploit in turn. Susan Snipe's sun reached high in the sky and her power grew with each year and every tainted mortal in her community.

Once Susan heard about and saw the biracial child of Mr. Grainer. She noticed, every few months, the car with dark windows came at night across her street to deliver Mr. Grainer's love child for an overnight visit. He seemed to be a nice young man and Mr. Grainer had done nothing to Susan Snipe. But, oh, how indiscriminate power simply begs to be used! The families in her neighborhood were not yet inclined nor practiced at tolerance, so she waited for an opportune moment. It came that summer at the pool. Her friends lay on lounge chairs lazily talking about their children. Joyce Simpson watched a friend of the Culver's boy. His friend was a dark skinned child of the migrant family who worked summers in the local nursery.

Joyce spoke, "Really I'm not sure they should let the Mexican kids in our pool."

"He's a guest of the Culvers, Joyce" Jane Johnson retorted.

"Still, you know how things get started."

Susan waited a moment to add her comment but not so long of a time lapse when the ladies would switch to talking about the new lifeguard.

"At least Mr. Culver didn't father that boy with a Mexican woman."

There was a thoughtful silence and Susan was sure to not look over at the women, who slowly turned their tanned faces with sunglasses toward her. Grist mills grind up corn and gossip mills turn observations into bagfuls of judgments. So life went for Susan. She enjoyed her hobby without repercussions for many years.

One winter, Susan felt spiritually inspired to plan a tour of some religious sites in Europe. She planned the trip with Mrs. Culver and Delia Townsend. Mrs. Culver wanted a break from her children and was fascinated by Lourdes. Delia worked in the parish office. She had an epileptic condition. She read the story of John Traynor and his healing from epilepsy in 1923. She hoped that, despite the millions of curious and uncured sick who visited Lourdes each year, she would be blessed with a healing at the sacred waters. They planned to travel to France in early June well before the flooding of tourists in Lourdes for the Marian Feast of the Assumption celebrated in mid-August.

The group added two more women from the parish, as well as Father Jerry, who would travel with them to Lourdes and then leave for additional time in Italy. Father Jerry was a perceptive man. Susan once brought him some baked bread for a student Mass and when they chatted in the rectory lobby, she noticed that he looked deeply into her eyes. She felt he gazed into her soul and she squirmed a bit before saying she had to run and pick up the kids from school.

On the plane trip, the group decided to switch seats with other group members every hour or so. Susan sat with Mrs. Culver first, then Delia, Mrs. Trimble and Spencer Mahoney. She leaned over to talk in barely audible voice with Mrs. Culver as they exchanged knowing looks and whispered innuendos about the stewardesses and other passengers. For the last three hours she sat beside Father Jerry. This time, he wasn't peering into her eyes. They talked of parish business and Father Jerry gently steered the conversation to talk about their destination.

"Mrs. Snipe, what thoughts do have about going to Lourdes? You must be excited to go there."

He half-heartedly paged through the American Airlines magazine. Susan looked out the window, seeing if the long bank of clouds leading to London might help her answer.

"Well I don't need a cure, if that's what you mean. I just thought I should see some holy places before I get too old."

"I see" Father Jerry glanced up at her, and then reached for his cup of water.

He seemed thoughtful and then replied.

"I wonder if everyone who goes to Lourdes, including priests and other religious, are somehow hoping for a change in their life. If not a physical cure, then perhaps they hope for some light to move their soul—a spiritual renewal perhaps."

Susan laughed and said, "Well Father, talk is cheap. We'll see if the Good Lord has plans for our little group."

Father Jerry's face quickened into a pleasant smile and he answered, "I'll say a few prayers that we all find healing of some kind."

After arriving in Heathrow the women with Father Jerry transferred to another flight to Lourdes and arrived late afternoon on the next day from their departure date in Louisville. Father helped them get settled in their rooms. The women were happy to rest and save the Grotto for the following day. Susan roomed with Delia. While Susan tried to nap, Delia seemed nervous, looking out the windows. She slipped outside after twenty minutes and Susan was grateful to be able to sleep for a few hours.

Susan awoke with the key turning and Delia walked quietly into their hotel room.

"Are you awake, Susan?"

"Yes" said Susan, stretching on the bed. "Where did you go?"

Delia put the hotel keys on the dresser and looked at Susan via the large dresser mirror.

"Well...I took a walk."

"—We promised each other to wait to go together to the Grotto!"

"No, Susan, I didn't go early. I had to go to the Basilica and I wanted to be very prayerful to prepare for tomorrow. It will be a big day."

Susan sat up on the bed and reached for her glasses.

"I don't think it will be a big day for me, but I hope you..." she hesitated, not knowing exactly how to wish her luck. So many seekers doubtless were left with some vague spiritual boost, well short of the handful of documented dramatic cures.

"That's okay, Susan. I know what you're thinking. And I didn't just pray for myself."

She turned around to speak directly to Susan.

"Not everyone needs a body healing. Some folks need something...more important."

Susan looked puzzled, tossed her head and hair and said, "Well you have a good attitude, Delia. I'll enjoy the fresh spring water, at least."

The group reassembled at seven PM and walked past shops and the post office. They found a little place called Le Magret and took their time having appetizers, wine and dinner. After eating, they walked some more and went into a shop filled with religious items, tourist trinkets and water containers of all sizes for capturing the precious liquid.

Father Jerry, a little flush from four glasses of wine, held up a five-liter bottle and said, "I'd better stock up for all the folks back home."

Susan let slip a quick answer without thinking, "Yes Father, so many in the parish need saving."

He set the empty white plastic jug down on the table and smiled at her. But it was an odd smile. Maybe he was thinking again or praying for someone.

The next day clouds hung overhead and the hotel shuttle took all of them directly to the holy site. They were there early, before eight AM, and there were only a few dozen of the faithful waiting at the walk to the spring. Susan looked in the faces of people who were all ages from teens to seniors and looking like they came from every kind of country. They seemed expectant, hopeful but rather serious.

Maybe they'll lighten up after they get their water and go back home Susan said to herself.

Spencer, Mrs. Culver and Mrs. Trimble held hands and rushed on, with Delia and Father Jerry holding back.

Father Jerry asked Delia, "Do you want me to walk with you there?"

She smiled and looked in his face and nodded yes. They walked together and Susan followed behind them. Susan stopped at a bench, wanting to give Delia and Father Jerry some relative privacy at the well. An older woman wearing native clothes walked near her bench, returning from the well. She seemed familiar with the path, turning the corners without looking. She looked at Susan and stopped.

"Bonjour, Como allez-vous?" Susan didn't know what to say. She didn't speak French.

"Bonjour, Madame" and added, "I'm sorry, I don't know how to talk with you." The woman smiled.

"Then I will talk in English. You are from America?" Susan smiled, "Yes".

"I have been coming here for forty-five years" she looked into Susan's eyes.

"But...you haven't found a cure for...what ails you?" Susan looked surprised.

"No, Madame, I come to give thanks for my being saved from a life of sin." The woman smiled again, nodded her head and left Susan alone.

At the Grotto, Susan arrived just as Father Jerry and Delia finished. The other ladies took a different path over to the Basilica. Father Jerry supported Delia, as she was smiling but seemed to be tired when they walked passed her. The tide of tourists had ebbed and Susan found herself alone at the Grotto. She listened to the gentle gurgling of water. She walked up to the black rock and spread her hands on the water, liking the massaging motion of water over her fingers. She heard another sound behind her, some whispering and saw another group of tourists approaching. For some reason, though, even though they were yet a hundred feet away, she clearly heard their whispers...

Who is that woman? Is she a cripple?

Why does she hug that wall? Maybe her sins make her reach for support.

I saw her in the restaurant last night. She flirted with the priest.

She talked with the gypsy woman back at the bench. I bet she is here to get water for her fellow witches.

Susan's mouth opened in shock and she pulled away from the rock, uncertain what was happening. She quickly pulled her little empty bottle out of her pocket to fill it at the fountain and leave as quickly as she could. When the group was almost to the Grotto she heard more whispering:

Why is she in such a rush? Did she put poison into the pool?

Look at how she is dressed and her hair all messed up. She no doubt has come here regarding some terrible sin. Perhaps she has cheated on her husband.

Susan's hands shook as she capped the bottle. As she looked at the group, men and women speaking German, she was doubly surprised to see all the faces smiling at her, despite their slanderous thoughts. She stumbled passed the group and a few women looked back at her and spoke. Once again, she could clearly hear and understand their words:

I saw her at the Hotel Saint Jean last night. She was with a group of women. Do you think they are lesbians?

She is an American, so dreadfully dressed. Why can't they wear nice clothes for travel?

Susan's feet took her to the Basilica but wherever people gathered, she heard them whispering about her. She paid for a taxi to go alone to the hotel, grateful that her group returned to London the next morning. But even the taxicab driver had whispered thoughts about her.

She travels alone, yet wears a wedding ring. Will she meet someone at the hotel? Perhaps she has a French lover?

At the hotel, through the afternoon, Susan drifted in and out of a restless sleep. Delia and the others returned. She told Delia that she wasn't feeling well. But Delia seemed renewed with greater energy that Susan had ever seen her display. She claimed that something had changed.

"Susan, it's so exciting! I know that water cured me of epilepsy. When I get home to Louisville, I will have some scans and that will prove that God touched me here!"

Delia moved herself to Father Jerry's room, where they were singing praises of joy and praying the rosary all night.

The return trip was difficult for Susan, trapped in the airplanes for two flights. She couldn't bare to sit next to Delia and for hours and hours she heard whispering, even when she looked and didn't see people talking. They talked about her, saying mean unfair and baseless things. It didn't help that she looked so worn and tired.

Back in Louisville, Susan tried to make sense of what happened at Lourdes. Delia claimed she was now cured of her affliction but she instead was put upon by some mysterious cruelty.

Maybe, she thought, *this is what schizophrenia is like. I'm going crazy!*

But deep down, Susan Snipe knew her mind was astute as ever. The spirit of Lourdes had taken Delia's burden and to keep some sort of perverse balance, placed what she perfectly well knew was a custom-made curse on her. The snippets of gossip she so easily placed on others had returned to test her soul. But how long would the whispering last?

Car Rider

I don't usually give someone a ride in my car. In fact, I think it was ten years ago, in Western Kentucky, when I last picked up a hitchhiker. He was a harmless young man who carried a didgeridoo made of fire-darkened PVC pipe. He was headed back home to the Northeast, for a hippie gathering. Still, I was relieved to drop him off in Lexington at Interstates 64 and 75. Sometimes it's safer to be driving alone, since loneliness can be an easier problem than...well, you'll see.

Mike Lopez worked as a counselor during the school year. For six weeks in the New Mexico summer, he held the position of assistant director at a Christian boys' camp near Silver City. The problems of the families and children in south Albuquerque were typical of a lower socio-economic community—drugs, alcohol, teenage sex and gangs. Mike worked as a social worker at La Raza Community Center. But he enjoyed taking a break from urban worries during June and July at the rustic camp in the Gila Wilderness. He felt, although the kids were a very similar mix of Hispanic and Indian, that he could be more of a father figure to the camp boys. It was informal, in the high desert mountains, with hikes, crafts and everyone pitching in to do meals and dishes. Mike often worked with troubled teens in Albuquerque but the campers at Mimbres Mountain Camp were younger, ages seven through twelve.

Mike particularly enjoyed telling stories to the children. Even if Mike had to leave a pile of dirty dishes at the lodge that called for a midnight washing session, he would run up from the lodge on the old logging road on Friday night, to be the featured teller. On a Friday in early July, thunderclouds glowed dull with flashes of lightning, as the storms faded away to the east near the Black Range. The older boys proudly went about their duties, as the earth spun the sun toward the west, placing piñon and juniper wood in a conical stack, ready for the fire. The camp folklore was well established, as the boys shared local legends well before the darkness arrived. The Indian boys brought tales of Navajo skin walkers, evil witches who flew as owls and the Hispanic boys held forth with stories of La Llorona, the woman who wailed for her children she herself had drowned.

"A rattlesnake is bad enough, when you're hiking through the arroyo by the old Indian ruins but three days ago I saw a dark figure down there. He kicked up dust, walking behind some big sagebrush. He disappeared when I looked again."

Johnny was a tall Anglo and he came from Truth or Consequences, where his father had a huge ranch. He was 17, one of the high school junior camp counselors. He lit the fire and the younger boys moved back as the piñon snapped and popped.

One of the young boys, Carlos, was Mescalero Apache. Although only ten, he commanded some respect from the others since he was tough and claimed his grandfather was a curandero.

He said, "Witches don't have to even look like people, they can roll around like a tumble weed, or fly up on a tall Ponderosa pine after they changed themselves to look like a hawk. My brother was canoeing down the Mimbres last spring with a church group. He saw some cattle on the ranch they traveled through. When he looked again, as they pulled around the hill—he noticed that one of the cows changed to a man. He said he was Indian but very dark and wearing a blanket poncho, like in the old days."

The group of twenty boys stood silently watching the fire, now reaching its peak, as zodiacal violet glow played with dark indigo sky. Soon the fire would subside and they would carefully check the short-cut log stumps for scorpions, dragging the stumps closer to the fire for seating to be ready for Mr. Lopez.

One boy spoke. "I don't mind knowing that there are...things, out there. But it makes me scared, knowing what they can do to you."

Mitch was eleven, one of three brothers at the camp. Their family came from Reserve, in the Tularosa Mountains. Mitch's older brother Pierce, a junior counselor sitting to his right gave him a frowned look and stared back at the now mellowing campfire.

Another boy spoke up. "What do you mean?" But all boys turned, startled, to hear jeans scraping past the junipers by the road.

"Hey, boys!"

Mike Lopez shouted, excited to tell stories to his waiting crowd. The boys cheered, forgetting Mitch's odd comment. Mike settled down on a large cottonwood stump, his favorite spot. He was prepared to tell six tales. He often either made up or rehearsed his stories on his drive down from Albuquerque. He usually took Interstate 25, south past Socorro, past Elephant Butte Lake to turn west on 152. The Interstate kept close to the Rio Grande and its valley. It was an ancient route for both Indians and the Spanish. The latter called it El Camino Real. It was their royal road from Mexico City to Santa Fe.

The boys nervously teased each other about who might scream or want to grab a friend and escape back to their bunk house. An owl called nearby and a quarter moon beckoned from the aspens to the south.

Mike waited for total silence and began his storytelling.

"One hundred fifty years ago, Stein's Pass, about fifty miles southwest of here, was a busy town on the stagecoach route."

Mike loved to weave true places and events into his stories, giving the boys both historical background and realistic settings for his more creative plot elements. He planned to tell two tales of pioneer or Indian ghosts, two stories of La Llorona, a bit of lore about the Plains of San Augustin with UFO's and a legend about a hitchhiker. He spun along his tales while the night darkened. Stars flickered beyond the red glow of the dying fire. The boys were hushed and somewhat tired by the time he got to the last story.

"My uncle Teo told me this story about a man who picked up a hitchhiker. It happened north of Espanola near El Rito. My uncle is a straight shooter and wouldn't make this up or believe a story from some drunk. He said this happened to a friend of his father, back in the early 1950s. This man's name was Salvador Espinosa and he worked his brother's ranch by the Rio Chama, not far from where Ghost Ranch is now. There are red hills that fall down to the Chama. It's a pretty spot but, like a lot of our land, very dry."

Mike glanced at the boys, who though tired, seemed mesmerized by the fire or by the now cold darkness. One by one they pulled closer to the fire. One of the high school boys threw a few aspen saplings on the red embers. The fire flashed up lighting Mike's face as he smiled and posed a question.

"I wonder what any of you all would do if you met the Devil?"

"I'd ask to see his little red tail, eh, vato?" Carlos joked and several boys laughed.

"Yeah, I guess so—that's pretty good, Carlito. But on a lonely stretch of road, a man feels compelled to help out a stranger, whoever he might turn out to be."

Mike added this philosophical thought to the boys stretched imaginations.

"It was April, leading up to Holy Week and the roads were busy with pilgrims walking north to Chimayo. You know, the pilgrims are people who promise to walk however long, a hundred miles or more. Some walk all the way up from El Paso to ask God to grant a safe return to their son fighting in the war or to give healing to their wife, or whatever. They come from all over and you can see them, leading up to Easter, along the Taos road. Salvador worked all day to bring in some stray cattle and was driving his truck about ten at night down a dusty road bordered by big cottonwoods.

"He rounded a curve near the old pioneer graveyard, made the sign of the cross and suddenly stopped to avoid hitting a coyote which dashed across the road. He thought it strange, though, as he had never seen a black coyote." Mike stopped in his story, noticing that three of the younger boys had curled up on the flat log and were already asleep. He smiled and went on.

"Salvador got the truck going again and turned onto the County Road thinking of his later dinner and how tired he was. He went for about five miles, going southeast toward Highway 84. He saw a figure walking along the right shoulder. Now he knew that the pilgrims did not walk at night, since there had been accidents. So he slowed down to see if the man needed help or a ride. Salvador and his truck came even with the man who was dressed in dark clothes and wore a western hat. The walker slowed to a stop and then turned to face him.

"It was hard to see his face, as there was no moonlight that night. But it seemed to Salvador that his face was old and leathery and lined.

He tried Spanish first, saying, 'Por donde va, senor?'

The man just stared at him. *Perhaps he is drunk,* thought Salvador.

So he spoke in English, 'Sir, can I give you a ride?'

The man nodded and reached for the door handle." Mike checked the faces of the boys. They were still paying attention.

"Was it the Devil?" asked Johnny. "My pastor says you can tell it's the devil if he smells bad, like sulphur."

Some boys chuckled and one offered another joke. "Maybe the devil likes his beans, and of course he'd smell up anybody's pickup!"

More boys laughed. It was a good break for the tension.

Mike continued. "Now, when you pick up a hitchhiker, you don't really have to talk. Maybe, sometimes, you don't really want to know who someone is or where they've been or where they're going. I won't say anymore about that. But Salvador got curious and of course, he wanted to know where to drop off the man.

He asked 'Where do you need to go?' He looked over at the man. He was a stranger. Most men from that area knew each other.

The stranger slowly answered, 'I have business in Nambe.'

Now Salvador was headed to Espanola but he wondered what a man was doing night walking and which business he might conduct at night. But he held his tongue and the stranger spoke next.

'You'd better get your truck fixed tomorrow.'

Salvador was surprised to hear this comment, and said, 'There's nothing wrong with my truck.'

The stranger turned to look straight at him and another car's lights lit up his face. Salvador saw his dark and very intense eyes and felt a chill run through his bones.

Fortunately, they had just come on Highway 285 in Espanola, and Salvador said, 'Sorry mister, I have to let you out here.'

The man replied, 'No problem, and thanks for the ride.'

Salvador watched the man walk straight across the highway, paying no heed to cars and trucks, walking a compass line to Nambe."

Mike stopped his story and stretched his arms. "Well I guess it's our bedtime, huh?" Mike asked the sleepy group.

"What—that's it, that's the end of the story?" Pierce demanded as he stood up. Some boys just started shuffling off and a few junior counselors poured water on the embers. Steam flew from the doused hot charcoals in angry hisses. Mike watched to see who stayed to demand a better ending to the story.

Johnny, Mitch, Pierce and Carlos lingered by the now dead fire.

"So that's it, Mr. Lopez? That's all that happened—come on, the little kids have gone—you can tell us." Johnny spoke for the group.

Mike sat back down. It was cold now and the constellation Hercules was swinging his club across the eastern sky. The boys stood as Mike finished the rest of the tale.

"Salvador was a little rattled. He drove straight to visit with Teo, my uncle, and they ate and drank until late that night. On the next day, Salvador went to work as usual. He had to drive up the low road to Taos and his truck brakes gave out on a sharp curve below Embudo. It took weeks before they were able to pull his truck and body from the Rio Grande rapids. My uncle only repeated this story once, to me. He told no one else."

"But I don't understand, Mr. Lopez, he gave the Devil his ride, he didn't blow him off." Carlos insisted. Mitch quickly corrected him.

"No, don't you see, he ignored the man's, or whatever he was, warning, by not getting the truck checked out." Then Pierce chimed in.

"It just doesn't seem that bad things should happen to good people."

"Yeah, I guess your right, Pierce, but who knows what our destiny is. Even Jesus got a raw deal from the Pharisees. Maybe the same devil turned him in—who knows?"

An owl sounded close by and Mike Lopez turned to go back to the lodge. The boys followed him in silence.

Mike saw the boys head to their cabins and he went

to check for phone messages in his office before going to bed. The red message light glowed in the dark and when he pressed 'play', he found it difficult to understand the words.

"Mike you'd better come back to Albuquerque, they took Mom to the hospital."

It sounded like his brother, but the voice sounded different somehow, like a higher pitch. Mike tried to play it again but in the dark, he missed the play button and hit the reset button—the message was lost. He stood there, feeling adrenalin pushing into his body and quickly decided he'd better drive back. Although he was tired, he knew he could still handle a drive of four hours. He'd pick up coffee in Silver City and because of the construction on Highway 152 he'd take the mountain route north and west through Glenwood and Reserve. It was a lonely stretch but it might give him time to pray and prepare for whatever was happening in Albuquerque.

Mike wrote a note for the director. They had no big plans for the weekend and some of the local boys went home anyway. He quickly walked to his Ford Explorer and turned to leave the camp as three owls on the picnic bench silently watched him leave.

He felt better stopping for coffee and drove out Highway 180. The first hour and a half went quickly as he approached Reserve, the logging town and moved on toward the east side of the Continental Divide. Next he had the open desert, the Plains of San Augustin, which stretched on toward Highway 60. He knew when he reached Datil that he'd be over halfway. It was windy over this stretch and this was the same area that he talked with the boys about, telling stories earlier that night of strange flying craft. He flew along at 75 miles per hour.

But before Horse Peak, he slowed down to focus his tired eyes because some dark shapes were crossing the road. He figured it might have been a group of cattle that escaped their ranch fences. He came to a halt about ten yards before what turned out to be a group of tumbleweeds, being lazily blown past the highway. One tumble weed blew away from the group and landed with a scraping noise under his car.

That's when Mike saw him, walking toward his car on the left side of the road. He seemed to come out of nowhere and the man walked up to the driver's side window. Mike was in shock as he rolled down his window.

"Hope I didn't scare you, mister. I'm trying to get up to Socorro. My jeep broke down two miles north on 603."

Mike just stared at the man. He was dressed in jeans and had a leather jacket. His face showed him to be about thirty years old. Mike quickly thought that anyone that could help keep him awake in this faraway section of desert would be a welcome traveling companion.

"Sure hop in—do you have any gear?"

"Nope—I have a duffle bag with the jeep but it's nothing valuable." The man answered and climbed in the front passenger seat.

The tumbleweeds blew by and were lodged on the west side of the fence, off the road. But as Mike pulled his car away, the one below his car seemed to scrape along for miles.

Mike commented. "That one just won't let go."

"Hmm..." was all the man said. The man talked quietly.

He seemed pleasant and Mike felt better having some company. But he did say a few strange things. He said he liked to play. He said he had a friend that traveled with him.

"Is your friend camping with you on this trip?" Mike asked.

"Not camping but he's here with us. He likes to play games too but he's not very nice."

Mike was puzzled and then, being a counselor, figured *this guy has an invisible friend.*

They passed Datil and joined a few more cars along Highway 60 and after forty-five minutes, arrived in Socorro. They found a Shell station open 24 hours, right before the Interstate.

"This will be fine, thanks."

"Good luck." Mike told the stranger.

And he drove away. The stranger watched as Mike pulled away toward the Interstate. Mike looked in his rearview mirror and saw him waving. Mike thought he was waving at him. But the stranger was waving to another rider, the one below the car, the one that had been hanging to the underside for 75 miles. That car rider slowly came up to the front grill. And then he slowly inched along the front hood in the darkness, being very flat. Mike was staring at his headlights fifty yards in front of the car and didn't notice the dark shape begin to cover the bottom of his windshield. Somewhere south of Los Lunas, the car rider moved quickly across the whole windshield and the blackness cause Mike to break in panic. His car skidded off the highway and rolled a dozen times. It took a while for someone, the next day, in the daylight to notice the skid marks. They found the car and Mike's body, surrounded by tumbleweeds that had blown in during the dark morning.

Namphuong

We never know where a wish might take us or how or when it may come true. Some wishes call for simple work, others for magic and others for the miracle of love. But those who have lived many years know that our wishes often involve the lives and efforts of many people. These can be both good and evil characters, taking different sides but acting in the same play.

A woman who lived in Vietnam wanted to find true love. She enjoyed her work as a teacher and had friends and family to keep her laughing. But she dreamed of finding a gentle man or prince. She wished for true love. She heard from her grandmother that if a woman sent a white dove at dawn towards the East, then it would return with a clue as to how to find the man she sought. She went one day to the market to look for a pure white dove but all she found were doves that were gray. She continued to look in her village for a white dove but she could not find it. One day, while shopping for her family at the market, she bought onions and fish from an old woman. The woman looked carefully at her and asked a question.

"Granddaughter, I see that you are a pretty woman, yet you have no husband. Why are you not married and happy with children?"

The young woman was surprised to hear this question from a stranger but she heard the same talk from her relatives. While she hesitated in her reply, a man ran through the market chasing a dog who stole a piece of meat. The running dog scared a flock of birds into the air and the old woman watched Namphuong's eyes following a white bird flying away from the market. The white bird flew alone. The old woman spoke again.

"My son can capture the white bird for you."

Namphuong turned to look into the woman's eyes and although she said no words, the older woman knew she wanted it to be so.

She said, "Come back at the new moon in two weeks."

Namphuong returned in two weeks and was indeed surprised to see the old woman's son had a white dove, captured and cooing in a small bamboo cage. The man smiled at her, handed her the dove and cage and left. Then the old woman spoke.

"I only ask for one thing in return. It is a request not for me but for my son. He struggles to work hard but if you can teach him another language then he will be successful."

The old woman instructed Namphuong to release the dove on the morning of the spring equinox. She told her how to pray and prepare so that the dove would fly safely and directly to find her love.

Namphuong agreed to the old woman's request for her son although she knew the school where she worked would not permit the poor man to enter and learn. So she made arrangements to tutor him after she finished her work days.

The land began to show signs of spring and the day came to release the white dove. Namphuong took incense and offerings to the graves of her ancestors and prayed for her dove to survive a great flight over the ocean. She fed the bird the best grains and greens and it was strong and ready. Namphuong bought a pure blue dress and awoke early in March to take the bird to the shore. The wind was cold and she feared the bird would be killed by falcons or blown far south.

Her hand shook as she took the white dove from its cage and said quietly, "I send my love to find my love— my heart will guide you there. Be safe and strong to journey long and return in calm air."

The ocean waves seemed to stop, the wind quieted for a moment and Namphuong tossed the white dove saying, "Go East—come back soon!"

She watched as the white dove circled three times. Namphuong was afraid the bird would not leave but then it quickly flew East above the sea and was soon lost in the clouds. As the sun rose, Namphuong returned home.

Namphuong spent several months trying to forget about the white bird and do her work. She tutored the old woman's son in English and often fell asleep at night, thinking of the dangers the dove must face. She went every evening to walk the seaside and often mistook the gulls and seabirds for the dove. But the dove was not to be seen and she began to fear that it was dead, drowned at sea or lost in a faraway land.

One weekend she went with her family to picnic by the seaside. It was June and they swam and played in the sand. Although they had a wonderful time, Namphuong sat and sadly looked at the ocean waves.

So many waves, so many lives, so many grains of sand, so many clouds, so many fish but where is my love, where is my dove?

Her mind drifted in sadness for some time until she was startled by the sound of children squealing in delight. They gathered around the picnic basket, watching a black bird trying to get into the basket.

Her father said, "It must be trying to get some food or make a nest."

A boy picked up a stick to swing at the bird and wave it away but Namphuong jumped up then to look at the bird more carefully. It was a dove, a jet-black dove. But when she looked into the dove's eyes, she realized it was her white dove returned, although she did not understand how it changed color.

"Please, leave it alone. I will take it out of the basket when we get home. It can replace the white dove I let go."

Her family and friends laughed at Namphuong but they let her keep the black bird.

Namphuong took home the black dove, wondering what happened to the bird, and feeling disappointed that the bird carried no message tied to its feet. She began to doubt that the black bird was really the white one returned.

How did it change color? Why didn't she receive a note with the bird?

She puzzled on these questions until one day when she decided to tell the old woman's son. She taught him for many months and after one session, she told him about the black dove.

"Show the bird to my mother and she will know what to do," he said.

So that Saturday morning, Namphuong pushed through the busy market with the bamboo cage and the black dove. When the old woman saw Namphuong, her eyes widened and she quickly spoke.

"You must take the dove to a friend of mine. She is a fortune teller. Do as she advises you."

Namphuong immediately followed the directions and set off walking across town to an area where many did not go. The streets were narrow and the feeling was dark. She knocked on an old wooden door, which had no window and a carved dragon, painted red.

She hesitated with her hand over the door, when the black dove made a loud cooing sound. A voice from inside then commanded her to enter. She slowly opened the door, as a strange smell touched her nose and she walked around tables with odd things. There were crystals, bowls of herbs and odd bunches of feathers hanging off old, dusty shelves. Namphuong was afraid and she could feel, in her chest, a tightening. Her mouth became dry as she walked toward the mesmerizing voice of an old woman.

"You have a bird to show me but it is not the bird you think it is."

Namphuong rounded the corner of a shelf full of wooden tablets painted with odd characters. She stood before a woman who sat at a round table with one open chair. She had a black dress and a kind face. Her hands reached forward to take the basket.

"It's not the white dove I sent out?"

Namphuong set down the basket before the woman. She sat down on a green, lacquered chair with woven seat. Both the chair and seat creaked and she realized many had sat before the wise woman. The woman's face was long and her white hair framed black eyes. Namphuong felt that looking into her eyes was like staring into the heart of another creature.

But what kind of creature looked out from those dark eyes? Was it a crow, a dragon or something more distantly removed from human contact?

"My name is Tuyen and I am a reader. I understand what people dream, what they cherish in their heart and what they fear. But the passion of their feelings is the vehicle for their own destiny if they will move decisively on my advice. Some do not act and fear leads to a shrinking back into darkness. But they do not know that darkness must be faced whether they walk forwards or backwards. You—"

Tuyen stopped, tilted the left side of her head up, listening to a sound Namphuong did not hear. She watched the old woman, who seemed to tune into another world, another reality. Tuyen gently took the black dove out of the basket and Namphuong was shocked to see many of the feathers fallen off. The bird seemed sickly and she was afraid her dream would die with the bird. Tuyen retrieved a bundle of feathers and set them as a sort of nest on the table. She lit a bundle of herbs and waved the odd smelling white smoke over the dove and feathers.

"We must wait in darkness to see what the bird will tell us."

Namphuong felt her eyes open as the darkness expanded with each candle Tuyen blew out. They sat in silence with barely a muffled hint of an outside world to remind them that they were in a city, not far away in a mountain retreat...

"I am Acilino" the bird spoke with a male voice, deep and confident. Namphuong's mind did not fully agree that this was indeed happening. She felt the darkness around her was thick and pressed upon her chest like the blackness of a cave.

"Tuyen you have well chosen to place me on a bed of eagle feathers, for that is my true form to which I will soon return. I am from a land across the sea and I flew back to visit my master. He is the love who this woman seeks. My master is held in a prison. I flew to his window where we talked before the wizard's wand sent dark fire to kill me. The bolt of darkness turned me black. I fell back, barely keeping my flight away from the rocks, falling into the sea. From there, an albatross swooped down, intending to eat me. But she realized who I am and my mission and she carried me on strong winds back to your shores."

"Stop speaking now, Acilino" said Tuyen, as she touched the black dove with a soft caress. "I know your story and what you must now do."

Tuyen reached inside her dress pocket and pulled a crystal which, even in that dark space, gave a white, wispy light from its point. She wove the light around the dove, as a spider might weave silk around its prey. She set the crystal down, made some motions in the air, making symbols that Namphuong could not understand. Tuyen then lit a candle on the table, and as the yellow glow slowly lit their faces, she saw the dove had changed into a small eagle. Its feathers were newly formed and Acilino stretched up his wings, ready for flight. Tuyen asked Namphuong to carry the candle and they walked out to release him into the night air.

Tuyen looked carefully to make sure all the people were inside, with their families at dinner. She threw the small eagle into the damp smoky wind. He spiraled directly up, circled three times and was lost into the low clouds.

Tuyen then turned to Namphuong, who could see, even in the dark that the old woman was smiling.

"Go home now but return here at the full moon of August."

Namphuong walked home, carrying the empty bamboo cage, her shoes clicking on cobblestone streets, dampened with evening fog. Many questions teased her mind. *Did the man I seek first send the white dove to look for me? Will the eagle go to find a way to help him out of prison? What can I do—an ocean away from him? How can I hope to fight a wizard or understand the efforts of a sorceress?*

She seemed no closer to her love than when she met the old woman in the market. Once home, she laid on her bed and while staring at the cage, cried until sleep blessed her sadness with forgetting.

And the eagle flew above pine forests, catching a cool wind to float away from the coast toward a rocky peak in the mountains. Acilino landed on a wind-bent cedar just at the edge of a flat clearing, where a tall figure stood before a fire. The wind grabbed hot sparks, flicking them into a snow bank where they hissed until silent.

Without looking behind, the tall woman dressed in black said, "You should not have come here, eagle." She then turned slowly and moved toward the eagle and tree, smiling mischievously, pulling a long staff from under her cloak.

"Your brother could not kill me, and neither will your magic find a mark, for I am protected." The woman stared, eyes narrowing to look inside the eagle's soul.

"I carry the strongest light and unstoppable force of a messenger bringing true love to its own." Acilino added.

"Ha!" She cried out, "Foolish is love, futile is the force for good and folly is the end of men and women."

"And you, Tien, are not exempt from the foolishnesses of humans?"

The woman frowned and said, "I cannot help you."

"But that is not true" insisted Acilino. "In your pocket you hold the key to a man's freedom."

Instinctively, Tien reached into her left side pocket to touch a gold neck chain. Her eyes no longer saw the eagle, tree and mountain. Instead she saw her mother, she and her brother, escaping the city as a witch hunt brought death to their family. She indeed knew that this precious jewelry, shown to her brother, would free Namphuong's man from prison. As she fingered the gold, she became a little girl, laying in her mother's lap and gazing at her mother's neck, hearing a sweet lullaby.

Tien turned away from Acilino and walked toward the fire, saying, "There is no rescue for men who have killed our own."

"This man has not harmed the mountain witch."

He insisted, "How do you know that the child of Namphuong and Nantan will not be another in your line of healers—to return the strength of the spirit people to man? Will not your favor, your gift, bring you a blessing that you may not now understand?"

The wind lowered as both the eagle and woman watched the moon rise above a distant lake. Tien felt a great sadness she could not contain, her face contorted as she tried to fight off tears. And then she fell beside the fire, crying without shame. Acilino flew over to offer her the touch of his wings, the warmth of a friend. Hours passed before the eagle flew back into the night, carrying the gold necklace in his beak.

In mid-August, as the drowsy hot afternoon began, Namphuong left work early to walk home and eat lunch. She got off early in order to prepare herself for her full moon meeting with Tuyen. Namphuong sat in the shade of her house garden as her mother finished lunch to bring to her.

She had weeks of disturbing dreams, when she saw a man, her lover, meeting death by many terrible ways. The wizard usually killed him off, whether by torture, starvation or casting him out onto rocks at the edge of the sea. But in each dream, she was able to look in his eyes and she felt his strength, his patience and hope that he would survive.

"Are you going to see...that woman, again?" Her mother asked, bringing rice, chicken and noodle soup. She frowned and added, "Nothing good comes from dealing with a witch."

Namphuong looked at her mother, worn and rugged from field work, serving a family and showing in her hands and face the challenges of decades of difficult years of war and disappointments.

"I need to finish what I started. I need to know...if he can be found." Namphuong took the plate of food and ate, while staring at the green garden and a cat sleeping under their plum tree.

Her mother shook her head and walked away, saying, "Young women are so often foolish."

Early that night, Namphuong combed her long black hair and dressed to travel to visit the seer. Her uncle walked with her across town, as neither spoke and the full moon touched a red, low cloud in the east. A large bird flew above and before them as they neared the old neighborhood, ruined palace stone walls to their left with busy merchants hurrying home.

He left Namphuong at the red dragon door. She waited for him to walk out of sight around the corner of houses and she waited still, staring at the carved red dragon. The dragon seemed alive, moving and its eyes looked straight into her soul. Its shiny scales caught the moonlight and it seemed to move off center, flexing its wings for flight. She shuddered, closed her eyes to shake off the moving image and reached to open the wooden door. Carefully walking into the long dark hallway and toward the woman's receiving room, Namphuong felt apprehension creep along her skin. She came up to the table but saw both chairs were empty and Tuyen was not in sight. There was a sealed envelope and also an open letter addressed to her.

It was a short note signed by Tuyen and read, "I've been called away, but here is a letter for you to read. It is from Nantan, the man you seek."

Namphuong picked up the envelope, felt its rough paper and moved her fingertips over the dips and bumps of the red sealing wax. The seal left the simple outline of a dragon. Namphuong eyes watered, she felt her body shake as she sat down and reached for a knife on the table to break the seal and read her letter. She pulled out a single folded sheet, and heard something fall out with the paper. It was a simple gold chain.

The letter read, "Namphuong, I want to thank you for your love and faith which has brought me out of difficult circumstances. There are others who helped release me from prison and death but your wish started my salvation. I am in your debt and I would like to personally thank you..."

As she saw below his signature, "Nantan", she suddenly heard a man behind her speak.

"Hello, Namphuong."

In the shadows, a tall man spoke and said, "Don't be afraid."

Namphuong spun around, grabbing the knife to hold out before her.

"No," he said, "I am Nantan but I am now just a form to talk with, my body is faraway."

Puzzled, Namphuong slowly lowered the knife.

"Tuyen is coming to bring me to you but this figure you see is a shadow of me so we can talk until I can travel to see you."

And so Namphuong and Nantan talked until late, when he said goodbye and she again sat by herself at the table. But she was no longer alone and as she walked home, a bright moon at zenith, her face and heart smiled with happiness of love which again found itself.

Moving Graves

Nobody with honorable intentions wants to dig up the deceased. We all deserve a peaceful rest in the land of the dead. But sometimes, coroners, police investigators or suburban sprawl demands workers with backhoes dig up friends, family or the forgotten. And if the coffin is forced open, we just hope there are no...unpleasant surprises.

Dust devils spun across County road 1570 in Franklin County, Kentucky, as a blue pickup followed curve after winding curve past hedge apple, elm and walnut trees bordering the two lane road. It was a late, dry summer and Malcolm Switzer drove to meet a work crew at Cedar Lane Cemetery. Malcolm's thoughts drifted within his mind as his eyes watched the road for cars or farm tractors. But on a mid-September Thursday, early afternoon, there were no school buses or traffic at all. Malcolm was free to mull over the near-finished job of moving the little country cemetery.

No one wanted to disinter the remains of 34 souls but the best route for the water pipeline from the Ohio River to Lexington, going through four rural counties, had to go right through Cedar Lane. The cemetery, unlike most other graveyards in the country, was closer to a creek than a ridge. Tall cedar trees, gray bark and limbs storm-broken below the twenty feet mark marked the perimeter of the cemetery. The graves, at least those recognizable as markers, hailed back to 1827. No doubt, there were older unmarked plots amongst the outlying weeds or lost below the dried green bluegrass.

Malcolm turned from the two-lane blacktop onto the gravel and dirt cemetery lane. A pair of County employees just began to dig into the last remaining plot. It was the grave of a friend and Malcolm decided to wait in his truck and eat lunch before walking over to inspect the digging.

Todd Johnson was buried fifty years before, when he and Malcolm were 12 years old. They played football together and spent many days hanging out, walking the big family farms not far from Cedar Lane. But friends who are close can have violent and sudden falling outs.

"Malcolm!" One of the workers was outside his truck, walking up to talk. Surprised, Malcolm set down his sandwich and opened his door.

It was Tim Howell, who said, "We saw you there in your truck. We found something interesting just four feet down. Thought we ought a show you what's down there." Malcolm, with a look of concern, walked with Tim to the open rectangular hole. There was red clay earth piled to one side. He looked over the edge to see fieldstones lining the bottom.

Tim took off his hat to wipe his forehead with a red, faded bandana, "I sure don't know how those stones could have gotten down there. My Father dug Todd's grave and I can't imagine he would have put any stones on top of Todd's coffin. It's almost like someone dug in here sometime since then and put stones to keep him from getting out."

The other digger, sitting in the backhoe, sat with a stone face, as smoke from his cigarette drifted into the blue September sky. He didn't lift an eyebrow. Malcolm stared into the grave, thinking about another September day fifty years before. Todd and he had a fight the week before and Malcolm felt betrayed by Todd. Todd let slip a comment about Malcolm's interest in other's boys. Malcolm decided that he had to stop a threat from ruining his life. Malcolm looked for powdered rat poison in his shed and put a pile of the deadly powder on a low crossbeam in his barn. Later that day, Malcolm lured Todd into the barn to play their jump from the hayloft game. But then Malcolm walked Todd over to show him a large wasp nest. When Todd bent close to look at the nest, Malcolm, from the other side of the beam, blew hard and the dust flew into Todd's face.

Malcolm laughed hysterically and Todd wasn't sure why his eyes stung and he was coughing so hard. The next day, Todd was unable to respond at home or at the hospital and the end came quickly. An autopsy revealed the poison but no one ever suspected he was killed by Malcolm's calculated and cold-blooded actions. Malcolm pretended to grieve and soon put the incident behind him, finding a busy life in school, family and career. He justified the murder as the necessary eliminating of the weak from a brutal society of haves and have-nots.

His flashback was interrupted, as Tim, puzzled look on his face, said, "Uh, Malcolm?" Malcolm looked up, startled back to the moment.

Tim repeated the question that Malcolm didn't hear, "Should we go ahead and clear out the stones or do we need to call someone on this?"

Malcolm quickly, vigorously shook his head back and forth, "No need to call anyone, just clear out the rocks and get the coffin up. We've got to have the land cleared by tomorrow morning."

Tim shrugged, as the other man restarted the backhoe. Malcolm, looking a bit dazed, walked back to his truck to drink some coffee.

As the men pulled out rock after rock, Malcolm wondered about what Todd's life might have been like if he lived. He shuddered at the thought he might have lost his good life if he didn't silence his friend. Malcolm looked over past the backhoe to see Todd's limestone monument leaning against a cedar. For a moment, he thought he saw Todd himself, sitting on the tombstone. Malcolm froze, foam coffee cup almost to his lips. He watched the image fade, sure it was a memory from long ago. But the hot coffee did little to take away an odd chill he felt, a chill to his bones.

Malcolm was again lost in his thoughts, not realizing how much time it took the two men to clear rocks and pull the coffin out of the ground. The sun, as if weighted by the sorrow of souls being removed from their resting place, hung sadly toward the western hills. He quickly got out of his truck, walking back to the gravesite. There was a very stiff breeze now, gusts swaying the cedar trees in circles.

Tim noted, "Sure looks like rain will be coming in tonight. We got this digging done just in time."

The other worker started to steer the backhoe over to the flatbed truck near the County road.

"You gonna wait then on the hearse? 'Cause Cain and I need to get the truck and backhoe back to Frankfort now."

Malcolm stared at the coffin. He felt this was his moment of truth. He felt a perverse need to open the coffin, talk to Todd's dead body and either apologize or make excuses. It didn't make sense but what does make sense in our lives. They heard Cain honk the horn for Tim to go.

"Yeah, sure, it's running late. I'll wait here." Malcolm barely glanced aside at Tim who waved and walked to the flatbed truck.

Malcolm's eyes were fixed on Todd's coffin. *You stupid bastard,* Malcolm thought, *why didn't you keep your mouth shut? For all these years I've kept a secret that has nearly made me crazy.* Malcolm looked up, seeing the men disappear down the County road, headed east to Frankfort. *I've got a good hammer in my trunk. I'm going to open this coffin.*

Malcolm walked back toward his blue truck. The dust spun around him as he reached inside his trunk to grab his hammer. *No one needs to know about the rocks,* Malcolm thought. *No one needs to know I killed you.* Malcolm smiled and just then a gust of wind pushed his head against the trunk door. It gashed his forehead and he stumbled back, ignoring his bleeding head to walk against a wild wind back to the coffin. It seemed that clouds came from nowhere and he thought he heard the rumble of thunder.

Malcolm swallowed hard in his dry throat, pausing before prying open the coffin. He looked again at Todd's gravestone not believing he saw a rat perched on top. *Must be blood from my forehead dripped into my eyes.* Malcolm worked feverishly to pry open the old coffin before sunset ended. Orange light lit up the cedar trees and the wind seemed to hold its breath while he leveraged the lid open. The coffin was out of the grave hole and rested on top of the ground, gray and black but turning red and violet as the sun threw its last rays to the west.

He pushed over the heavy lid, staring in disbelief at the empty coffin. Malcolm saw only dust, a gray dust in the form of a man.

"How could the bones have turned to powder so quickly?" Malcolm nearly shouted aloud. Just then a wicked cold wind whipped the entire pile of remains upward, flinging the death powder into Malcolm's face.

"No!!" Malcolm screamed, clutching his face and falling backwards over the fresh dug pile of earth. He lay backwards, blinded from the deadly powder, choking and then turning over to try and throw up. Malcolm raised himself, intending to run to his truck to get water and splash it over his face. He dashed blindly out from between the cedar trees, directly into the hearse's front grill.

People say that Malcolm, discovering the empty coffin of his friend went crazy with unresolved grief. People commented on how tragic it was that Malcolm was killed by the hearse as the Cedar Lane Cemetery claimed one more dying soul. People wondered about the boyhood bond between Todd and Malcolm.

People don't know the half of it.

Strange and Wonderful Thing

Death is a friend whose visit is usually postponed until late in life. The gift then that death brings is often release from suffering or the timely termination of a long life. But when death comes much earlier, perhaps a different gift is offered. In the eyes of the young who are dying we may just see a reflection of our heavenly home. And visitors from faraway places sometimes have very unique gifts.

Joshua Mason was eight years old and he was dying. His Mother and brother kept cheerful watch despite the energy-draining efforts of the previous five months. Joshua had leukemia and after months of chemotherapy and then bone marrow transplants, it was clear that Joshua had at best one week left to live. He was tired from near countless trips to the hospital and sat in his bed at home, waiting.

Sitting, bald-headed, in bed while his Mother talked on the phone and fixed lunch for his baby sister, Joshua stared at the ceiling. Models of spaceships hung from hooks. They moved slightly back and forth, as the fan above pushed warm air downward. It was January and the corners of his window to the backyard were framed with frosty lines.

Joshua drifted in and out of sleepy images as his

Mother spoke, "I suppose, Dr. Caldwell that it's harmless to let him believe those things are happening."

The voice on the other end of the line was Dr. Bill Caldwell, psychiatrist.

"It's not unusual for a child of Joshua's age to exhibit what we call magical thinking. And of course, with the extenuating circumstances of terminal cancer, we could expect that he wants to both escape from pain and translate denial into fantasy. It might not be helpful at this time to challenge or confront what he tells you about these...unusual events. Every child wishes their thoughts would manifest immediate reality, particularly a reality that brings pleasurable happenings."

Dr. Caldwell waited then for Mrs. Mason to reply. She was practiced at stifling the urge to cry and Dr. Caldwell, despite being 15 miles away at the University Cancer Center, felt her upwelling and unspoken frustration and grief.

He said, "Why don't you just play along and enjoy talking with Joshua about his stories? Since it seems your time is very precious now, consider it a fun game. Besides, this is exactly where your son is at now, how he best knows to deal with his disease and what it has done with his life. If it makes him happy and does no harm, then I think you both can just let it go."

"Thank you, Dr. Caldwell I've got to go now. Sarah wants lunch."

Mrs. Mason hung up the phone and looked in on Joshua, who seemed to be asleep, with a slight smile on his face. She returned to the kitchen and cut her daughter's sandwich and sighed.

When Joshua opened his eyes, there was a girl standing by his bed. His visitor appeared to be about 16 years old, slender and with long blond hair. Her green eyes delightfully balanced a wide smile, and when she spoke, there was almost a musical sounding of light bells. She wore a shimmering dress of violet blue, her hands reached over to touch Joshua's forehead.

He turned to smile at her, saying, "They don't believe that you visit me."

She laughed and turned away to set a model spinning.

"Not all grownups know everything there is to know, Josh."

She walked over to the window, waved her arm, and the frost disappeared, snow melted from the flower boxes and tulips rose instantly in bright colors—yellow, red and peachy orange. He giggled and sat up in bed to look at the flowers. It was a strange and wonderful thing to see.

The girl looked at Joshua's happy eyes and said, "I'll be back later. Have a nice visit with your Grandma. Don't worry about Sarah."

The moment she disappeared, Joshua heard his Mother shout out, "Oh, God, no Sarah!"

Mrs. Mason rushed into Joshua's room, shouting, "I'm taking Sarah to the emergency room—she swallowed something. I'll call for Grandma to come over and watch you!"

She left quickly, picking up Sarah, who was breathing with difficulty and ran out the door. Joshua carefully got out of bed, walked down the hallway and closed the still open door.

He grabbed a blanket from the living room sofa and went into the kitchen to pull a soda can from the fridge. His Grandmother Jean drove up in her big ol' car just ten minutes after his Mom left. He smiled as she walked in the door, flush from rushing over and searching his eyes for any worry or fear.

She gave him a hug and said, "Your sister is alright. They'll be back after some errands."

"Hi Grandma" Joshua added, "Did Mom tell you about my friend?"

"No, Joshua, but hold on while I call your Mom to tell her I'm here." Grandma Jean called Joshua's Mom while she pulled a stuffed animal from her big purse.

"This is for you" she whispered.

It was a small cuddly bear. Joshua had plenty of those, lots of stuffed animals from people he knew and folks he didn't know. Actually, he was a little tired of stuffed animals and people who only smiled at him.

Hanging up the phone, Grandma Jean remarked, "Say, Joshua, who put the bright plastic flowers on the windowsill? That's a fun thing to do in the middle of winter!"

Joshua answered, "It was Karen. She's my new friend. She comes to visit, and people don't see her. Those are real flowers she made grow up."

"Oh really?" Grandma Jean stopped cleaning the kitchen sink and walked slowly over to sit across from Joshua at the kitchen table.

"I wonder where Karen lives." Grandma Jean inquired, sliding some graham crackers over to Joshua.

Joshua picked up one and looked at it carefully while answering his Grandmother, "Karen lives in heaven. She told me that I'd like it there. They have cool toys and lots of other kids to play with."

Grandma Jean suddenly had a serious look on her face, a single tear in one eye.

She forced a smile and said, "We could all use a friend like Karen."

Joshua nodded, crunching down on his cracker. Grandma quickly got up and walked to the fridge to get Joshua some milk. She took her time, her back to Joshua, wanting to keep from crying. She swallowed hard, shook her hair back and pulled the milk carton and set it on the counter. She poured the milk into a glass.

Joshua watched her carefully, "Are you sad Grandma?"

She spun around, bringing him the milk and answering slowly and thoughtfully with a few more tears in her eyes, "Joshua, I am sad that you have cancer and I'd be sad at first if God calls someone like you to go home to heaven. But I'm also so very happy that I have you for a grandson and I will always love you, wherever you or I may be."

They talked for a while longer. Mrs. Mason called to say they were headed home and Joshua asked his Grandma to read him a story before he lay down to nap.

He curled up in his bed and Grandma Jean read one of his favorite books, *The Gift of Nothing*. The late afternoon winter sunshine was bright and filled the room with rays. When she finished, he was asleep. She sat on the side chair, watching him breathe. She then got up, patted his bare head, looked out the window and saw the tulips. One tulip was drooping in the winter's cold air.

Strange, she thought, *plastic tulips wouldn't droop.* She walked toward the hallway, stopping just on the way out the door, when she fancied she heard a light, musical laugh. It sounded like a girl's voice. Grandma Jean then heard her daughter and granddaughter in the garage and she rushed out to help them carry in their bags.

Joshua was very tired and he slept through dinner. While his Father and Mother played with Sarah, television sounding in the background, Joshua slowly opened his eyes.

He knew Karen was there and he said, "I told Grandma about you."

Indeed, there the girl stood, silent but smiling. There was a pretty light around her face. She looked at Joshua for a while. The voices of his family faded away. Joshua still felt very tired and weak.

"Are you taking me to heaven?" Joshua whispered. The light around Karen moved and glowed, pretty colors of blue and orange. He heard the sound like the seaside when waves come in and go back out. Joshua felt a rush of air pull him out of bed and he took Karen's hand and they flew up and outside.

And it was a strange and wonderful thing as they flew around the house, laughing, seeing the night's moonlight but not feeling cold. They flew down to look inside the big family room window, warm with orange light. Karen watched Joshua look at his family as they stood hovering, inches above the snow. He smiled and watched them for some time, until they left to get ready for bed.

And, the next day, Joshua's body was lifeless when his Father went to check on him. His family and friends prepared a lovely funeral for later that week. And those who loved him cried. They were very sad for a long time. But the love they felt for him didn't die with Joshua. And that was a strange but wonderful thing.

Ornaments

From ancient days people have made dolls and fetishes to create magic and put meaning into their everyday life. Examples include Native American kachinas, church statues, Voodoo dolls, religious icons and even the clothing of a lost loved one—all carry special meaning for the devoted. "Contagious magic is defined as the belief that objects that have been connected will have an influence on each other even after they have been disconnected." We can keep a link with someone even after they have left our life; although there may be times when we'd rather not keep that intimacy.

Jennifer was thrilled to meet Frank and right before Christmas, no less! What a lovely time to start dating and take in the holidays with a special friend. They met at an early December office party and exchanged phone numbers that night. He worked with computers and she managed a dental practice. They both lived in Lexington and soon discovered mutual favorite places—Joseph-Beth bookstore, Ramsey's restaurant, the Kentucky theater and more. Since they were both divorced and in their 40's with no children, compatibility seemed easy and fun.

On the second date, they went ice skating, flirting

with each other, holding gloved hands while gliding over the ice. Off the ice, taking a break, they sat on benches while children scrambled around them. Jennifer took off her wool hat and her mid-length red hair fell down. She swept it off her face.

"Oh, I've got to get my hair cut! It's driving me crazy!" Frank eyed her, knowing it could be tricky to agree with a woman's statement about her appearance.

She added, "It's just so expensive, not $11 like for you guys!"

He laughed with her, adding, "Well I can cut it for free if you want!"

Jennifer looked aside at him, smiling and saying in teasing tone, "I just may take you up on that!" That night, outside the skating rink, they first kissed. It was pleasant and passionate and Jennifer was happy. She emailed her sister that night.

I'll have you know that I'm not falling for him completely. He does have some faults. He seems very OCD, but I guess most computer geeks are that way. I like it that he is an artist and he likes the same music I do. But I guess we'll just have to wait and see how it goes. Jennifer's older sister, Dawn, was hopeful for her. But she also heard a few negative things about Frank, having worked with Frank's brother, and knowing Frank's ex-wife and one of his ex-girlfriends. Dawn decided to hold off on telling Jennifer about what could be just gossip.

The following Saturday Jennifer agreed to drive to Frank's home for homemade dinner and a video rental. Frank greeted her with a kiss and offered her rum-spiced Louisiana Lemonade.

"Go ahead and have a look around, make yourself at home. I'm almost finished getting the food ready."

Jennifer walked around Frank's small but well-furnished home. He had photos from his family, a nice collection of music and movies and items from his travels on tables and shelves.

"It's almost ready" he called from the kitchen.

"Smells wonderful and I didn't have to cook it!" she laughed.

Over by the front door on top of a pretty dark wood table, Frank had a Christmas tree. Jennifer saw Frank made homemade ornaments. There were about two dozen dolls, with simple clothes and made with realistic clay faces and hair. They seemed to all be female and the heads sported blond, brunette and brown hair.

"Any more lemonade?" Frank snuck up behind her.

"Oh, no, this will do me for a while. You've got interesting Christmas ornaments."

He reached out to touch one, saying, "Yes I made all of these dolls. They're very special, each one. But come on, sit down for dinner."

Jennifer reluctantly took her eyes off the dolls. They seemed to stare at her with glass eyes, as if wanting to warn her about something important.

The dinner was pretty good for bachelor cooking as Frank fixed food from his New Orleans upbringing. His Cajun cooking included shrimp Jambalaya, red beans and rice, followed by Missy's pecan pie. They relaxed after dinner on the sofa.

"I learned so much growing up in Louisiana," Frank said as he pulled up a coffee table for their feet to rest on. My great Aunt Dominique was Creole and I learned music, dance, culture and more from her.

He whispered, reaching for the video remote to turn on the movie, "She even knew some Voodoo."

Jennifer looked at him, puzzled and amused but the movie started and the evening flowed by. She left right after the movie, since she had to get up early on the next day, Sunday, to have breakfast with her Grandma and go to church. They agreed to meet again on Sunday afternoon at his place to take a walk in his nearby neighborhood park.

The day was sunny and they both talked about plans for Christmas. Jennifer was reluctant to get involved in meeting each other's families but did want to introduce Frank to some friends. They went inside Frank's for hot apple cider to warm up and chat for a while.

As they sat at his kitchen table, Jennifer itched her neck, saying, "Oh that long hair scratches at my dry skin in winter!"

Then she looked at him, got up and got a pair of scissors from his kitchen counter, walked over and put the scissors into his hand.

"Trim my hair."

"Yes, Ma'am" he said, smiling, asking her to show him how much to trim. He carefully cut off several inches, working to even up the sides, as Jennifer talked with her Mother on her cell phone. Not a lot of hair fell to the floor, as Frank took trimmed handfuls and set them on his table. When he finished, she gave him a thank you kiss and she excused herself to leave for errands.

"I'll call you tonight" she shouted on the way to her car.

Frank smiled and waved as she pulled her car out of his driveway and he went back to the kitchen to sweep up the trimmed hair. But instead of throwing away her pretty red hair, Frank held it lovingly, feeling the essence of Jennifer. He got out a wooden oval box, gently setting her hair in the box for keeping. He felt he captured her with the trimmed hair.

That work week was a challenging time for Jennifer as patients kept them working late getting in their dental appointments for the holidays. Frank claimed to be busy both at work and at home at night.

He reported, "Santa is busy in his workshop."

Then on Thursday night, Dawn called Jennifer to phone chat.

After catching up on family news and each other's work trivia, Dawn seemed to prolong a goodbye, finally saying, "Jennifer, I don't like to bust your love bubble but I think you should just know a few things about Frank. Actually, it's more about his ex-girlfriends and former wife."

Jennifer was laying in bed, half-reading a good novel, which she set aside to better listen.

"What do you mean? What are you talking about, Dawn?"

"Well…it may just be a coincidence but do you know that none of Frank's ex's ever found a steady boyfriend or remarried?"

Jennifer was silent, listening, as Dawn continued talking.

"I talked with Frank's brother, you know, the one who works at Lexmark. He said he hoped it would work out for you and Frank. He said he thought it was odd that after 18 years Frank's ex-wife hadn't even stayed with a regular date for long. And I talked to Sylvia, Frank's most recent ex-girlfriend. She names eight women who Frank dated and she said the same thing—no one including her has been able to keep a man."

"Dawn, that's just weird but it doesn't necessarily mean that Frank and I couldn't find a wonderful relationship." Jennifer stared at her dark bedroom window trying to imagine why all those women didn't marry or find a boyfriend.

"Maybe, Jenny, but Sylvia told me that he once kept her fingernail clippings in a box and that he had other things from his ex's—like a scarf, or pantyhose or locket of hair."

Jennifer sat up in bed, saying, "Really. Do you think he's into fetishism?"

"I don't know, Dawn, what he could be into, you never know. But just be careful and don't rush into anything, okay?"

After they talked, Jennifer sat in bed with the lights out, wanting to sleep but thinking over the previous several weeks. When she closed her eyes she saw the doll ornaments and they fell off Frank's Christmas tree onto the floor.

I must be dreaming now thought Jennifer. The dolls were scooped up by someone, a man, who carried them into another room, a dark room with red candlelight. One by one, he tied something around each doll and then tied all the dolls together. He put the dolls into a basket and then he put out the candles. It was dark.

On Saturday, Jennifer drove to Frank's house to pick him up to go together to a bookstore. But she was preoccupied with thoughts as she drove, thinking about Dawn's comments and suddenly finding herself at Frank's driveway.

It wasn't until her knuckles knocked on Frank's door that she realized *he's got my hair too.* At that moment, Frank opened the door, smiling and welcoming her into his house.

Jennifer walked onto Frank's living room rug but her head pivoted to his Christmas tree and her eyes scanned the doll ornaments, searching. And there she found it, a new doll—a pretty little female doll with red hair.

She turned on Frank, demanding an answer, "What did you do with my hair that you cut?"

Frank turned away, buying time to answer while he reached inside his coat closet for his favorite black leather jacket.

"Well I threw away the hair, of course," he lied.

Jennifer was numb, not knowing what to say next, whether to throw out angry words or just leave him. She decided it was best to just leave his house and they went out together to the bookstore. They browsed books separately, she headed to the travel section and he found books in the metaphysical shelves. But Jennifer could not remove the image from her mind of the new, red-haired doll.

While they were away, back at Frank's home, the Christmas tree where Frank's homemade dolls hung got very warm. Maybe it was an old set of lights or maybe the heater vent below the table put out hot enough air to combust the synthetic tree or maybe the nearby outlet shorted out. But that night, Frank's house went up in flames. When Jennifer returned with Frank, they found the firemen and emergency vehicles. She stayed just long enough to make sure his brother picked him up to spend the night.

And Jennifer no longer saw Frank for dates. And that year, there were quite a number of women,

Frank's ex's, who had wonderful new whirlwind romances. They all found new friends and lovers. Cupid's arrows found their marks. It was a very good New Year.

Happy Campers

Every summer our children are sent off to camp to have fun, learn to do crafts and appreciate the rugged outdoors. Some children are nearly forced by their parents to leave behind video games and social isolation in order to find some improvement in social skills. A number of adults claim their summer experience at camp dramatically affected them, pushing them to grow up, become a leader or leave behind the isolation of their nuclear family. One boy forever left his sheltered life behind but in a way that no one could possibly imagine.

Albert Bentley Carson was a child of privilege. His mother lyrically intoned his nickname, "A...B...C!" leaving a higher pitch in the final letter. She would say, "ABC your piano teacher is here" or "ABC your junior scientist friend is on the phone" and so on. Albert Bentley was only partially aware of his nerdyness. He certainly could see that he had a fraction of true friends compared to his 12-year old classmates. But he thought he was fully engaged in life, with computer, video games, books and chess. He was a bit pudgy with short black hair and, yes, the classic glasses that communicated "geek".

His parents, Julius Irwin and Evelyn Arianna, were

a bit concerned though with his lack of social involvement. Since Albert had no interest in sports, school clubs, or an extracurricular activity that involved more than two people, they consulted with one of the most highly recommended psychiatrists in town and also spoke with his school counselors. The significant adults in Albert's life hatched a plan to rope him into Boy Scouts, drama school and swimming lessons. His mother and father, ready to sit him down and inform him of his new life being thrust into the social world, were surprised themselves to suddenly deal with Julius' transfer from Albany, New York, to Los Angeles, California. Albert was saved from social embarrassment, as in April his family prepared to move. In early May they flew to their new home.

Albert escaped from the stress of worrying about re-entry into another, totally different school environment by spending spring happily building a few bridge models, online chatting with his buddy back in New York and reading science fiction fantasy. But his parents, determined to boost his confidence in relating to other boys and girls, signed him up for a youth camp that July in the San Bernardino Mountains. On June 30th, in the late afternoon, his parents packed his things into their Mercedes and they drove to Big Bear Camp, northeast of Los Angeles.

Albert was quiet, contemplating his fate, wondering just how much his future fellow campers would torment, tease, bully and relish making fun of him. When they left the freeway and headed into the foothills, he listed his liabilities: not an athlete, not coordinated, not a local, not handsome, not hip, not cool, no scars from knife fights or exciting accidents, not up on music...and so on and so on. Albert sighed, pressed his face against the window and decided he would have to just endure the four weeks. They pulled under an old Western-style wooden gate with a faded painted bear on the left and the camp sign on the right. There was a circular drive which, after driving three fourths of the way around, stopped at the administrative cabin. Some two hundred yards behind was a row of cabins and a few other large log buildings.

A smiling woman, in her late 40's, sat on the porch, waiting for the family to unpack and start saying goodbyes. She wore green shirt and pants, like Forest Service personnel. Sunglasses covered her eyes and her face was shaded under a cowgirl's hat. She walked over to greet Albert's parents. Mr. and Mrs. Carson were startled to see her close up. When she came out from the porch shade they noticed her face and arms had large patches of healed skin grafts. But they were polite and she was friendly, so they held any comment.

"Hi folks, I bet you're the Carson family. How was your drive? My name is Ashley Phoenix and I'm the director of Big Bear Camp." Mr. Carson chatted with Ashley while Albert argued with his Mother about taking a second suitcase, which held a portable computer with satellite linkup, video games and more.

"Actually, Mr. and Mrs. Carson, we don't allow any computers, video games and other electronic entertainment or communication devices."

"Well there you go, honey, I told you they wouldn't let you have those here." Mrs. Carson patted Albert's head while he set the suitcase back in their trunk, a disgusted look on his face.

"Are the other campers here?" Mr. Carson asked Ashley.

"Um, yeah, they're at the west campground. This is the east camp."

Mrs. Carson was cooing over Albert when his Father interrupted with a whispered, "You know we agreed this was better if we made the goodbye brief, dear."

Mrs. Carson kissed Albert on the cheek and was reluctantly pulled away by her husband. Ashley and Albert watched them pull away, chalky gray dust billowing up behind their blue Mercedes. The sun had just disappeared behind the tall Ponderosa pines.

Ashley set Albert's things on the porch.

Albert voiced his concern, "Is it safe to leave my stuff out here?"

Ashley laughed, "Don't worry Albert, we're pretty isolated out here, the only people that come out this way are lost campers who need help with directions."

She took Albert inside to show him the main cabin. He plopped down on a bench covered with black and white cowhide. Ashley sat on a willow wood chair covered with an old Indian weaving. A stuffed bison head looked down on them, its dark and mysterious eyes examining the newcomer. Albert began to have a creepy feeling. There were no other kids, no noisy obnoxious teenage camp workers. He looked to her, eyes squinting together, not sure if he could trust this woman.

"Where did you say the other kids are?"

"Look Albert, let me level with you. We really don't have any other campers here." Albert looked stunned, then frightened, then a bit angry. He looked at the door.

"What do you mean? It's a summer camp, right? Lots of kids running around, doing stupid things, singing camp songs, making fun of...kids like me? What am I supposed to do out here for four weeks? They took all my computer stuff." He was indignant. He eyed the phone.

"I should call my parents now. They can pick me back up in just a half hour. Believe me they don't want me to be alone." His word hung out in the air, but he realized they were not his words really but his parent's words.

"Albert, we last had kids here five years ago. The owners got into other businesses and they haven't yet sold this property. They let me live here as a caretaker and your parents are the only ones who called to send a kid to camp this summer. They said all the other camps were full, since they checked it out so late in the spring. I hated to let them down."

Albert eyes were wide with disbelief. He shook his head and rolled his eyes, "Great, are you gonna keep me captive here for four weeks?"

For the first time, Ashley took her eyes off Albert, looked away at a picture on the back wall. It was an old black and white group photo of about 40 campers and staff.

She stared at the photo and sighed, saying, "You know, I was a camper here a long time ago. There are worse things than being away from your family for a few weeks." Ashley turned back to address Albert.

She stopped, looked into his eyes, and then something flashed across her face.

"Albert, I have an idea. My guess is that your parents forced you to come to camp, right?" Albert grunted in agreement.

"Okay and I bet you'd like nothing better than to hang out at home with your computer stuff, right?"

"Yeah," he said. "So?"

"Here's the deal—you can call your folks, go back home and they will probably send you to day camp in L.A. for the next month or make you take up some sports lessons or who knows what. Now, I would like to get my office set up with a nice computer, you know, get back to the Internet age. How about I take the money your folks paid, we go into town and get computer stuff for both you and me. You can stay at the staff cabin right by my cabin. And you can spend the next four weeks taking it easy here, with some time to just get my office updated. What do say?"

Albert looked outside. It was now dark. His parents wouldn't really want to be called. This was a chance to both please his parents with camp attendance while not having to deal with a month of peer hell. He could easily set up both Ashley's office computer and his own cabin.

Ashley stood up and reached out her hand to shake with Albert, "Deal?"

Albert hesitated just one more second, then smiled and said, "Yes Ma'am, I think we can do business together!"

"Great," said Ashley, "let's get your things to the cabin right behind here and while you settle in I'll get your dinner ready."

Albert suddenly had the feeling that camp was going to be just fine, something he could handle. They each carried a bag, walking out the side, with a view to the west. In the violet-red afterglow of the sunset, Albert saw a line of torches bouncing along the distant lake.

I thought she said there aren't any other campers here Albert wondered but he entered his cabin and since he was hungry, quickly got his things unpacked.

"Come on back to the Buffalo Cabin as soon as you're ready," Ashley turned and left.

Albert ate well with Ashley that night and he enjoyed hearing a few stories of the misadventures of campers over the years. Ashley told him how one group initiated new campers by putting a turtle under their bed sheets.

After dessert, she sent him to his cabin, saying, "Just let me know if you need anything, I'm right here. Don't be afraid to wake me up if there's an emergency. We'll have breakfast at 7am and then leave for town to get our computer gear. I appreciate you being a good sport about this."

Albert smiled at Ashley but he wondered about her skin patches. He figured she must have been burned kind of bad some time.

"Good night, thanks for dinner," he walked the 25 feet to his cabin and got ready for bed.

His cabin had electricity, since it was a staff cabin. Ashley told him that the other kids' cabins, just down the lane, were primitive. But when he drew back the curtains to behold the dark night and bright stars, he noticed that each cabin had a light in it. *I wonder who is in those cabins tonight.*

He just started to drift to sleep when he heard a scratching on the front door. He hoped the sound would go away—maybe it was a raccoon but he didn't have any food in his cabin. Albert slid out of bed, a bit afraid to open the door. He stood inside, waiting until the scratch came again. Then he flung open the door and there stood a smiling, tail wagging dog. In the background, he saw Ashley silhouetted in the open doorway of the Buffalo Cabin.

She called out, "I see you met Trigger. Do you want me to call her back? She'll be wanting to stay in your cabin and keep you company. It's up to you, Albert." Albert looked down at his canine visitor, her wet nose already in his hand. She was a mutt but mostly a border collie.

"It's okay," he said sleepily and the two went inside—Albert to his bed, and Trigger who lay down nearby. He slept well.

The next day, Albert discovered that Ashley had another dog, a German shepherd named Bravey. After breakfast she took him in her old Chevy pickup to a computer store in San Bernardino. They were plenty busy the rest of the day as Albert set up Ashley's office with a new computer and accessories, loading software and getting the modem online. They took a break before dinner for a short hike to the lake.

As they sat on a picnic table by the lake, looking at dragonflies darting back and forth, Albert commented, "I saw hikers with torches out here last night. Is there another camp around? You told my parents there are kids at west camp."

Ashley looked at the lake and after a few moments answered, "Well, there were kids at the west camp but that was a long time ago back when I was a camper here. There were so many kids we had two separate groups. It was a fun rivalry, going back and forth, sometimes stealing things from each other's cabins. That was in the 1970's."

Ashley suddenly hopped off the picnic table top, "Come on, aren't you hungry?" Albert followed her down the path, kicking rocks and watching a set of crows on top a burned Ponderosa tree.

It was cooler that night, as a storm approached from the north. After dinner Ashley lit a fire in Buffalo Cabin's fireplace. She left him to hang out by the fireplace while she went into her office to write some email on her new computer. Albert stayed there to enjoy the fire, reading a book he found. It was a big, coffee table size hardbound book, titled, "Big Bear Camp: Fifty Years of Adventure and Friendship". He read through the first section until his eyes grew heavy. Then he paged through a later chapter which had group camper pictures of every year from 1952 until 2002. He had one hand on the book and the other petting Trigger. Bravey only moved around with Ashley.

Ashley returned to the main room bringing hot chocolate from the kitchen for Albert and her to drink.

"So what do you think about our camp here?" Ashley handed Albert the hot drink. The wind was getting stronger outside and they both stopped to hear the Ponderosas sway back and forth, creaking and dropping dead little branches.

"It's pretty neat. I saw the group photos. Which one are you in?" Ashley smiled, picked up the book and went straight to 1970. She pointed to a smiling blond girl who sat in the first row of about three dozen kids and a half-dozen staff.

"I was ten years old and so excited to go to camp. I came with my older brother, Derek, who was fifteen. He actually worked as a camp counselor over at the west camp." Her eyes looked sad. Albert wanted to ask her why she looked sad when both jumped as there was a knock at the door.

"Stay here, I'll get the door. Maybe someone's lost in this storm, trying to get back to town." Ashley opened the door and Albert couldn't see who was out there. But he heard the rain splash down and a bright flash of lightning pushed in through the curtains from all around the cabin.

A man's voice said, "You all are going to lose electricity. You'd better light the lanterns now."

Albert only heard Ashley answer, "Okay."

Then she closed the door and headed to the side table to light the two lanterns. He didn't hear a car drive away. Just then, the brightest lightning struck very close by and a minute later the lights went out. Ashley already had the lanterns ready.

She brought one over to set by Albert, saying, "They should have the power back on later tonight. This lantern is for you to take to your cabin."

Albert waited about fifteen minutes, until the rain stopped. During that time he stared at the fire. Ashley finished drinking her hot chocolate. He didn't look at her, but he wanted to ask her questions—questions about the other people who seemed to be around. Then he walked out, followed by Trigger, to his cabin. Although the wind swayed the trees and there was a fog near the ground, he again clearly saw lights in the other cabins in east camp.

He felt a chill and thought *something weird is going on here. I like Ashley and I think I trust her but we are not alone.*

When Albert settled down in his bed, he decided the next evening he would walk down to have a look at who was in the cabins at night.

The sun was strong the next day and the sky blue, the air cleared from the storm. The electricity had come back on in the early morning. After a breakfast of eggs, toast, and sausage, Ashley asked Albert if he wanted to stay around camp when she was gone doing about an hour of errands. Albert said he was fine, Trigger would keep him company.

After Ashley pulled out, Albert waited about five minutes and then walked down to the east camp cabins. He had gone by them a few times before but didn't get a close look or try to get inside. He walked to the first cabin, which had a faded sign. The sign was obviously a project for some camper. The wood burned letters read, "Little Bear Cabin". Albert walked up to the door but it was padlocked from the outside. There were weeds showing that no one had been taking care of the cabins. When he looked inside the windows, he saw a layer of dust atop the furniture. Albert walked down to the other four cabins, all were locked. None showed any sign of use.

When Ashley returned, she got very busy with her chainsaw, cutting up fallen dead trees and piling the wood in her truck to haul to Buffalo Cabin. After lunch, Albert felt bad she worked alone and he pitched in for several hours. As they took the last load, he looked over at Ashley, wondering about her and what happened with her life.

He felt bold enough to ask, "Um, Ashley, do you mind if I ask you about your"—he stopped short and was suddenly quiet.

She turned off the truck when they arrived at the cabin and turned to him, saying, "You mean the skin on my face and arms?" Albert bit his lip, feeling guilty for bringing up the topic.

Ashley stared ahead, east, toward the plains. She had a dreamy look on her face.

"You know, there are forest fires sometimes in these mountains. I barely escaped with my life from a bad fire." Albert felt uncomfortable and they unloaded the wood in silence.

That night, the moon came up bright. After dinner Albert read in his cabin. He saw the lights go out early in Buffalo Cabin. Ashley was tired from the physical work that day.

He waited until about eleven PM, he whispered to Trigger, "Shhh, if you don't bark you can go with me."

Albert put on his shoes, jacket and carried a flashlight as well. He slowly and quietly opened his cabin door, walked on the grass to avoid snapping twigs, cutting through behind the main lane toward the east camp cabins.

Yes, he said to himself, *the cabins are lit! There is someone there.* The first two cabins had lights and he could actually see a few figures moving around inside.

He walked straight up to the first cabin, ready to knock on the door but it was open and a young man saw him at the doorway.

"How are you doing, camper?" The boy was a teenager and two boys his age sat at chairs by the table. They were smiling, talking.

"Come on in!" The first boy introduced himself.

"My name's Derek." Albert barely heard the names of the other two boys, as he suddenly realized Derek had the voice of the man who warned Ashley about the electricity going out.

"Oh you came to our cabin last night, during the storm," Albert noted.

"You bet, buddy, I always keep an eye out for my fellow campers." Derek smiled a sly smile.

"But which camp are you at? I don't see anyone at these cabins during the day?"

Derek turned to look at his friends, "Right" he said, stretching out the word and offering a chair to Albert.

"Would you like to sit down?"

Albert sat down and started noticing how the boys were dressed. They just had tee shirts and shorts, even though the night was now cool. They didn't seem very tan for summer campers.

"Actually we are at the west camp. We just come here at night to make sure you all are okay."

Albert brightened, "I haven't been to the west camp. Would you take me there?" Derek looked at his friends for a moment and they raised their eyebrows.

He looked back at Albert, "Sure, why don't we go now?"

They started out the door. Out of nowhere, the three had lit torches, which helped Albert better see the path. They followed a well-used trail around the lake, past a meadow, up a long hill and to the base of a mountain. There were six cabins and all were lit, with dozens of campers outside, talking, playing guitar. The west campers waved and greeted Albert and his three new friends.

After an hour, Albert noticed a group of girls surrounding another girl who seemed upset. She had red hair and a pretty red beret. She was crying.

Albert asked Derek, "Why is that girl crying?"

Derek turned from chatting with another camper, looked over at the girls and remarked, "She's homesick. I think we'll be having her parents come and get her tomorrow."

Albert agreed, "Yeah, I think after three days I kind of miss my Mom and Dad."

Derek smiled. After a while, Derek saw that Albert was tired and the two boys and Derek hiked Albert back to east camp. He thanked the three and as he walked to his cabin he noticed something strange. Trigger was there waiting for him. But she started his walk with him.

It seemed, when he thought back, that he couldn't recall Trigger going into the cabins with him. She must have stayed there.

The next day, after breakfast, Albert read books Ashley brought from her uncle's house. He lived down the road and had interesting books on the history of the mountains. Albert noticed he spent much less time on the computer than at home. He learned the trails, liked to help Ashley with some of the camp work and was learning the constellations. As they ate lunch, Albert thought it was okay to mention his trip to the cabins and west camp.

"I couldn't sleep," he fibbed, "and I went out for a walk. I saw lights at the cabins and I went down and talked with some boys there."

"Really?" Ashley perked up, setting down her coffee. "Who was there?"

"Well, I'm sure you know them, since they seemed pretty familiar with east camp, though they stay over at west camp." Albert said with authority.

"One boy was named Derek and I met a few others too." Ashley seemed thoughtful.

"You know, Albert, I think I should show you something. Let's go on a hike."

Ashley finished putting away the dishes and they took some water bottles. She led Albert down the lane, past the cabins and lake and down the same way as he went the night before. But the cabins were shut up, and there was not a trail past the lake. Ashley took a stick and swung back tall grass. There were trees filling the meadow and when they got to where he remembered west camp...there was nothing, only a few darkened pieces of lumber.

Albert walked over to sit on a rock, frowning and trying to make sense of the night's hike and this day hike. He shook his head, while Ashley looked at him, studying his face. When Albert looked around, glancing behind the rock, he saw a tattered and dirty red beret, barely visible in the dirt, moth eaten and old. Then Albert felt dizzy and the next he knew he was up against the base of the rock, with Ashley leaning over him, splashing water on his face.

"I shouldn't have let you stay here. Or I should have told you from the beginning." Ashley was talking but Albert was not sure he heard her.

"I was here in 1970 when the forest fire came through so quickly. There were wildfires from here to the coast. Over a half million acres burned. Hundreds of homes were destroyed. I was staying at east camp. We got out but my brother Derek and another 18 campers at west camp were caught in the fire. They died that day but I guess you know by now, that their spirits have not left."

Albert sat looking past Ashley at the empty campground. He couldn't believe he walked and talked with ghosts the previous night. Ashley helped him up and they walked back in silence.

Back at the cabin that night, Albert asked to call his parents. They spoke for thirty minutes and Albert told them about camp, working with Ashley, Trigger and the other kids he met.

"Mom and Dad, they're the nicest kids I ever met."

Mr. and Mrs. Carson were so proud of their son, the happy camper.

The Closet

Grown ups sometimes play with children's innocence, offering up such folk tales as the Easter Bunny and Santa Claus. The Tomfoolery can double back on the adults, with children claiming they see the Boogeyman under their bed or faces in the shadows of their room. "It's just your imagination!" exclaim frustrated parents, who usually see such matters in black and white. Actually, what they usually perceive is that which is seen in the light of day, not the darkness of a closet.

Ten year old Cynthia Hodgson did not mind moving to a new home. Her parents and the movers did most of the work. Her Mother asked her to watch her younger brother Jerry while they unpacked the many cardboard boxes. Since it was a warm spring day, Cynthia took Jerry by the hand and went out to the back yard.

The Hodgsons' new home was a large, three-story brick built in early the early 1900's in Old Louisville. They moved from Shelbyville to be closer to both parents' jobs in downtown Louisville. Their house was off St. James Court with other Victorian Mansions on each side and pretty period gas lanterns out front. Cynthia took two-year-old Jerry to explore their new back yard.

The yard was small but a dogwood bloomed above brick-lined flower beds.

"Hey, Jerry, look—somebody left their sandbox back in the corner!" Cynthia spoke enthusiastically to Jerry, bending down to smile broadly in his face. She pulled at some ground vines, clearing greenery off the pretty white sand.

"No trucks," said Jerry, indicating that he had no trucks or cars to play with inside the sandbox. Cynthia looked at one of the back windows. She saw her Mom in the second floor kitchen busy taking out dishes from moving boxes. She didn't want to bother her now.

"Well, Jerry, since this house is so old, I bet there are some neat things forgotten and buried in the sand. We can be like explorers and dig to find some marbles or an old car." Her brother nodded, let go of her hand and started wandering about to find a stick. She watched him look around the yard.

He's a nice brother, pretty much she thought. Cynthia was glad the school year was over. Sometimes her classmates didn't really understand her. They all wanted to talk about boys and teenage things. She still believed in fairy tales and once in a while saw things that other people couldn't see. At their old house, out in the country, Cynthia saw a black woman. She was large and had a happy face. When Cynthia was six years old she got sick for five days. Her Mom was at home but busy with her real estate calls and checked on her every two or three hours.

Cynthia remembered how her Mom came in late in the afternoon of the fifth day, saying, "I'm sorry I haven't come in very often to see how you're doing."

Cynthia answered, "Its okay, Mom, that nice lady has been taking care of me."

Her Mom looked puzzled and finally slowly said, "Honey, it's just been you and me at home today."

But Cynthia insisted, "No Mom, that nice dark lady with the white scarf, she's big and friendly. She always visits me when I'm sick." Her Mother frowned but said no more.

Cynthia bounced out of her remembering, seeing Jerry rooting through some weeds, "Careful of snakes in there, Jerry!" She was nearly over to pull him away when she saw he had a rusted metal shovel, missing its wooden handle, in his hand.

"That's great, Jer', now we can dig for treasure in our new sandbox." Cynthia helped Jerry carry the shovel-head back to the sandbox and after he tried some digging, she stepped in to work the shovel down into the sand.

When she had a nice pile, she told him, "Okay now we can put our hands into the sand—like this—to feel for something." She heard her Mom call for lunch just as Jerry squealed with delight. He found two old metal cars, which he started zooming around the wooden edge of the sandbox.

Her Mom called again and she answered, "We're coming Mom!"

Three things happened rather quickly. Her brother started walking across the yard toward the back door. Cynthia, while looking at him, felt something in the sand. She pulled it out, brushed it off and saw it was a white porcelain doll's head.

While inspecting the baby doll's face, Cynthia heard a girl's voice say, "That's my doll!" Cynthia looked up and saw no other girl in the yard.

Her Mother picked up Jerry from the back step saying, "Come on, we've got lunch ready!"

One more thing happened as Cynthia walked to the house. For some reason she looked up at the third floor window and saw a girl, dressed in white, frowning at her and pointing a finger at her. Or maybe she pointed at the doll.

It's not surprising that Cynthia's Mom didn't believe there was a girl upstairs in their new home. But her Dad gave her the benefit of the doubt and walked up to make sure nobody was up there. At least, he didn't see someone there.

As they settled in, both Jerry and Cynthia enjoyed exploring and playing in their new home. Her Mom took extra time off from work to spend with them and to get things organized. Cynthia liked the multi-story house, the tall ceilings, the old wooden staircases and the green grassy court out front. The previous residents modernized the kitchen and painted the rooms in different warm colors. The first floor had a parlor and office space for her parents, the second floor had the kitchen, dining and living rooms and the third floor had three bedrooms.

Cynthia and Jerry played with the dumb waiter, sending dolls and toys up and down from the upstairs laundry room to the second floor bathroom. Jerry found two boys to play with who lived on their court. Cynthia started getting bored. There were no new neighbor friends and school was several months away. There was a boy her age and she saw him come out once in a while. He bounced a basketball in the backyard next door.

Cynthia liked her room with all her clothes, furniture, toys, dolls and play horses relocated from their old place but she didn't like her closet. She felt scared being near her closet. The closets in this older home were large things, framed in dark stained wood, tall and deep.

She asked her Mom to read her a book at bedtime, delaying her time alone. When her parents left her to sleep, Cynthia usually swept up the covers over her head and hoped to quickly fall asleep. Even so, she heard knocks and bumps from her big closet. After a week she also heard voices. They were muffled voices, as if two or three people held a low conversation.

At first she thought she dreamed about the girl. It was the same girl she saw in the window. Cynthia often woke up to see her playing on the floor with her horses.

The girl looked up at Cynthia, saying, "My father knows all about horses. He owns lots of carriages." Cynthia, drowsy in the night's darkness, watched the girl just fade away.

In the morning light, Cynthia was curious to see which of her dolls or horses were moved from where she left them. It happened every night. Something was always somewhere else. But most of all, Cynthia didn't like waking up with her closet door wide open.

"Mom, I saw that girl upstairs again in my room. And the closet door is open when I get up. I know we closed it before I went to bed!" Cynthia indignantly reported to her Mother.

"Honey, I'm sure your Daddy or I must have left the closet door open. Please don't worry about the closet. There's nothing in there that can hurt you."

"But Mom, I saw that girl again!" Cynthia watched her Mother make sandwiches for their trip to the zoo.

"Maybe we need to find you a new friend from the neighborhood. What about the boy next door? Have you said hello to him?"

Cynthia let out an exaggerated sigh and rolled her eyes to the heavens. She shook her head and walked out of the kitchen to plop in the sofa by the wide front windows. She heard a giggling and opened her eyes wide to see the ghost girl make a funny face then run up the stairs. Cynthia leapt from the couch to race after her, seeing her turn the corner on the upstairs landing. She reached the top, spun around and chose to look first in her bedroom.

When Cynthia rushed into her room she saw no girl but the closet door just clicked shut. Cynthia reached out to open the door, hesitated a moment and opened the large wooden door. It creaked as she slowly opened it and she saw only her clothes on hangers. Everything seemed to be in its place.

The sunlight through her windows lit her bedroom and pushed through into the closet. In the daytime the closet almost looked normal. She noticed a slip of white below her hanging clothes, near her black shoes.

"I know you're in there," Cynthia spoke to the ghost girl, adding, "You can hide or disappear to the others but not to me." She loudly cleared her throat for emphasis.

Slowly the girl in white pulled back the hanging clothes and stepped out from the back of the closet. She walked past Cynthia, who felt a cold chill over her body. Then the girl simply dissolved into thin air while whispering, "Stay away from the closet at night."

Cynthia sat on her bed for a while trying to understand what just happened. She stared at the closet for several minutes then got up and closed it firmly.

In late July a large thunderstorm rolled in one night. Cynthia was even more scared of the closet. For three weeks after the ghost girl led her upstairs, Cynthia heard the closet voices get louder. It sounded like people arguing, their voices rose in pitch and intensity. She thought she heard two men talking. Cynthia asked her Mother to let her keep her Grandmother's rosary at night. On the night of the storm, Cynthia tried to sleep but instead her thoughts raced. Flashes of lightning threw odd shadows across her room. Outside, an ambulance wailed and dark shapes of trees flung about.

She heard the floor creak. She bravely lifted the covers. There was the girl, white in face and dress. The girl seemed to want to talk.

"What do you want?" Cynthia challenged her. She was a little scared but she also felt sad for the girl, stuck in time with no family or friends.

"Can I stay in bed with you?" The girl's face was both honest and scared.

Cynthia ventured another question, "What's the matter? Why are you afraid?"

The girl slowly climbed onto to Cynthia's bed, sitting atop the covers with her back to the wall. Her face seemed blank, as if she was lost and alone. Cynthia felt her own cold left foot that was near the girl.

Then the girl spoke again, "The men in the closet

won't let me leave to go see my Mother. When nighttime comes they come up from the secret tunnel and stairs to the closet. They want me to go with them but I hide in the house and I don't go near the closet."

"Where is your Mom?" Cynthia sat up in bed and offered the girl a stuffed bear. "What is your name anyway?"

"My name is Mary. My Mother went away to the hospital a long time ago and I miss her. Sometimes I think I hear her call my name but I can't find her."

Cynthia looked at Mary and thought carefully. She tried to make sense of her story. Just then a very loud clap of thunder made both girls jump. The closet door swung open, Mary screamed aloud while Cynthia froze in terror as a dark shape rushed out of the open closet. As the shape moved toward Mary, Cynthia heard her Father's voice in the room.

She looked back toward her bedroom door and saw her Father who said, "We heard you scream. Are you alright?" He turned on the light and moved into the room. Cynthia turned towards Mary but she was gone.

"Close the closet door, Daddy, it came open and something came out." Her Father touched her as he walked by, walked over to the door, which seemed to have difficulty closing.

"Hmm, I'd better check this tomorrow and fix the door so it stays shut." Cynthia watched her Dad struggle with the door. He finally jammed it closed. He walked back to hug his daughter.

"Daddy, can I keep the light on?" Cynthia begged her Father.

"Okay just this time." He kissed her forehead and left the room.

Cynthia stared at the closet wondering what happened to Mary. Then she noticed something on the hardwood floors. There were dark footprints that led out of the closet. They went five paces to her bed and then...there were no more. Cynthia got out from her covers and bed and walked over to bend down to look closely at the dirty footprints. She reached out and touched the dark stuff. It was smeary, like coal dust.

The next day Cynthia felt that Mary was not around, whether taken by the closet men or hiding from them.

I wonder if I can find the way out of the closet to the secret tunnel Cynthia thought. Cynthia watched morning cartoons, since it was Saturday. She walked Jerry outside to his friend's house where there was a birthday party. She stayed to help watch him and took some pieces of cake for her family. After the party ended and the young guests left, Cynthia left Jerry to play with his birthday buddy. She walked home and saw the neighbor boy sitting on his front porch. She lived in the neighborhood for several months but hadn't spoken with him. He seemed quiet.

He looked at her as she walked up the sidewalk.

"Hi," he said. And she looked up surprised.

"Hi," she answered then added, "Would you like some cake from Martin's birthday party?"

"Sure," he said, getting up from the porch and walking over to reach out for a piece of cake. "Thanks." He looked away, seeming to pretend that he wasn't interested in her.

"My name is Cynthia. You can call me Cindy though." She looked past him to his house. "Do you have any brothers and sisters?"

He shook his head and then said, "My name is Alan." He walked back to sit on his porch and she followed him to sit there too.

He looked right at her then said, "I know your house is haunted. My friend Jason who lived there told me about the ghost. She's a girl about your age. Do you know about the secret tunnel?"

Cynthia un-wrapped another piece of cake for herself, eating slowly and shook her head no.

"You can get to the tunnel through my backyard cellar. A friend of my parents who is a professor at the University told them the tunnel was for escaping slaves."

Cynthia looked at Alan, wondering if she might trust him to talk about the ghost girl and her scary closet.

He finished the cake and said, "Come on, I'll show you the tunnel." Cynthia felt her heart beat faster. She looked next door and her Mom wasn't in sight. Alan waved from the space between their houses and she followed him to his backyard.

As he lifted the wooden cellar door he talked more about the cellar.

"We had a tornado scare four years ago and we had to stay in the cellar for 45 minutes. I was bored and moved an old wood telephone wire spool to sit on. That's where my Dad and I saw the entrance to the tunnel. I think the first family lived in both of our houses and that's why there are tunnel entrances from our cellar and from your house. Jason couldn't find the tunnel entrance from his house."

The two walked down into the cool dark cellar. Alan left the wooden door open and the daylight guided him to the light switch. He turned on the light and took Cynthia to the east side, pulling the wooden round spool away from the tunnel entrance. There was a wood plank door set flat on the ground with old limestone pavers around it. When he lifted the wood door she felt cold air push upward. Alan stood by the open tunnel door and looked at Cynthia.

She looked at his face and asked him, "So...have you been down the tunnel?"

"Well it's kind of narrow down there. And I'm not too excited to be in tight places, you know. I wasn't going down until Jason dared me to go one day. I went down just far enough with a rope connecting me to Jason. We found that the main tunnel entrance is actually under the old coal bin." Alan walked over toward the front of the court, south, to show her where the coal bin once was.

He lifted a large metal plate and Cynthia gasped, seeing wide stone steps leading downward.

"Oh yeah," Alan said, "This is interesting."

Cynthia barely heard her Mom calling but Alan said, "It's definitely your Mom. You'd better go. We can go down here together another time."

Cynthia walked from the cellar along the fence to U-turn to her front porch and inside her home.

That night in Cynthia's home it was very quiet. It was hot muggy evening and the sunset and twilight dragged on and on. Cynthia thought about the closet while she helped her Mom with dishes. Her Dad was busy and didn't have time to work on the closet door in her room. So the closet was still stuck shut.

Just as well she thought as she walked upstairs to the bathroom to brush her teeth. As Cynthia looked in the mirror she caught movement behind her. Someone walked into her room. She hoped it was her Mom or Dad...or Mary. Cynthia walked out of the bathroom and called for her Dad to read her a book. Her Mom got him from downstairs while she ran back down to the living room. Cynthia and her Dad walked back up to her room and she settled in her bed.

After her Dad read the book to her, she asked him, "Do you think there are ghosts?"

"Why do you ask?" Her Father replied.

Cynthia told her Father about Mary and about the tunnel. She told him about the night before and something coming out of the closet. She told him about the noises and voices. He listened quietly and asked her if she wanted to sleep with them.

She thought for a bit and said, "I think I'll be okay."

Her Dad read Cynthia another book and tucked her in for the night.

She lay in darkness and listened to her parent's wall clock. After 10:00 PM Cynthia heard her Mom get up to help Jerry go back to sleep. The closet was quiet and Mary was not to be seen. Cynthia hugged her stuffed bear close and pulled the covers over her head. She drifted off to sleep.

In the middle of the night her Father, not sleeping well, got up and went into his office to write an email to a friend of his who was a counselor. He asked advice about what to do regarding Cynthia's belief in ghosts. Then he slipped outside to take a walk in the court, pondering the issue as he walked in the cool summer evening. When he returned, he looked at his house for a while, wondering what could make his daughter scared. Perhaps it was a trick of the light, maybe it was Cynthia up from her bed but he thought he saw a girl looking out of the third floor window. His heart skipped a beat and he hurried back into the house and up two flights of stairs.

Mr. Hodgson opened the door to his daughter's room. All was quiet, the closet door was shut and there was no girl at the window. He went to the bathroom and got a flashlight and a screwdriver. He walked very quietly back to Cynthia's room to open the closet door. With some prying the door came open. He pushed her clothes aside and examined the floor and back of the closet. Evidently made at the turn of the 20th century, it was made of quality paneled walnut. There were no buttons visible to indicate a secret way to open the closet to hidden back stairs.

He knocked gently on the wood and it seemed to have a hollow resonance. As he held the flashlight and screwdriver in his left hand he gave the back panel a hard strike with his fist. The momentum of his hit pushed open the back panel and he went flying down into the unused and unseen stairs, tumbling down and falling for over thirty feet to a spot well below the ground. The hinged panel bounced back to close just as firmly as before. The closet left virtually no evidence that he was inside and fell to his death.

Cynthia was briefly awakened by the noise but she turned over and pulled her covers more tightly. Only one person saw what happened, Mary, who sat on Cynthia's bed and watched as a dark figure shut the closet door and pull back the clothes and hangers. Mary walked over then to take the plastic horses down from Cynthia's shelf. She set them on the floor and started humming to herself.

About the Author

Thomas Freese is a writer, storyteller and author. He currently lives in Louisville, Kentucky. Thomas Freese is also a counselor and expressive therapist.

Thomas has written over 100 articles, since 1999, for Lexington's Chevy Chaser and Southsider Magazines. His monthly feature is called "Day Trips", and highlights fun and intriguing local travel destinations. Thomas employs his own photographic talents in his articles and books. He illustrated another author's book, Shirley Hayden-Whitley's *Sometimes Life Ain't Sweet You Know*, (1994). His first book, *Shaker Ghost Stories from Pleasant Hill, KY*, was published in 2005. He followed *Shaker Ghosts* with *Fog Swirler and 11 Other Ghost Stories*, (2006) and *Strange and Wonderful Things* (2008). Thomas is completing his fourth book, *Ghosts, Spirits and Angels*.

Thomas Freese entertains audiences as a storyteller. He tells tales in libraries, story festivals, museums and bookstores, using animated voices from his collection of accents and characters. He plays guitar and harmonica, creating wonderful original songs, such as "Whatja Gonna Do With a Silly Kitty?", "All in My Head", "Porquois Song", "Lost Shoe Blues", "Stuffed Animal" and more. His story programs include Porquois Tales, Ghost Stories, Silly

Tales and Songs, World Folktales, Fairy Tales, Winter Tales, Origami Stories, Desert Stories and Urban Legends.

Shaker Ghost Stories

Shaker Ghost Stories is a collection of true experiences from the visitors to and employees at Shakertown, Pleasant Hill, Kentucky. Pleasant Hill has been over 200 years in existence and is one of the restored Shaker villages in the Eastern United States. The Shakers, or United Society of Believers in Christ's Second Appearing, worked diligently to create a Zion, or heaven on earth. Their founder, Mother Ann, encouraged them to put their "hands to work and hearts to God". While the Pleasant Hill Shakers have passed on, their legacy of spiritual devotion and material prosperity remains. The Shaker village is a peaceful place to visit and learn about Shaker life, to enjoy singing and overnight stays. Those who come find a spiritual touchstone in walking the land, hearing Shaker music and marveling at their craftsmanship.

Some of those who work or visit there have

discovered that some Shaker spirits have perhaps returned to Pleasant Hill. The collection of odd occurrences reported in Shaker Ghost Stories include mysterious singing, phantom footsteps, appearances and disappearances of Shaker-looking people, invisible helping hands and the sights and sounds of work and worship continuing at odd hours. The Shaker spirits seem to act much in character with their original dispositions—demonstrating faith, fervor and a guardianship of their homes and land.

Traveling East in 1990, Thomas Freese visited friends, looking to relocate from New Mexico. Thomas was intrigued by Shakertown and the lives and accomplishments of the Shakers. He moved to Lexington the following year and in 1996 became one of the Pleasant Hill Singers. While learning and performing Shaker music, he heard his new friends often speak of their "Shaker experiences", occasional and unusual happenings. Boosted by their encouragement, he spent the summer of 1998 taking notes and collecting accounts of the Shaker Ghost Stories. While returning for performances and singers' retreats, Thomas continued to collect Shaker ghost stories up until the publication of his book in 2005.

The chapters include an introduction, The Shakers at Pleasant Hill, "Are there any ghosts around here?", A Whirlwind, Women in White, The Mystery of Holy Sinai's Plain and The Shaker Experience.

Bill Bright, a former Pleasant Hill employee, tells of an amazing experience:

"It was in the winter of 1996 and Dixie and I were working in the village. She noticed that the candles from a candlelight performance were still in the windows of the Meeting House. Dixie decided that they needed to be put away so we stopped in there. I helped gather up the candles and Dixie went to put them in the closet.

"Since I was a bit bored, I walked over to a spot between the two front doors to sing a little. I was next to a gap in the wall benches, facing the back wall. I started to sing sets of three, descending notes (triads). Since I had spent plenty of time in high school band, I figured that it'd be a neat exercise to try the acoustics in the large room of the Meeting House.

"As I was singing, something appeared in the middle of the benches to my right, on the sister's side. For lack of a better explanation, it looked like a human form, very similar to the special effect done in Star Trek when they beam up somebody. It seemed to rise up from the floor to my height. At that point, the hair on the right side of my body stood on end, while the left side was not affected. I immediately got cold chills, like I had just walked into a meat locker. I just wanted to get out of there. I left the building immediately, quickly enough to make Dixie come out after me."

"She asked me, 'What's wrong?'"

"I told her what had happened and she suggested that I talk to Randy Folger, the music director. When I saw Randy, I told him about the experience and he simply asked me if I knew what I had been doing. At that point I had no idea. Then Randy asked me to sing as I had been singing in the Meeting House. After I sang for him, Randy explained to me that I had unwittingly been singing the 'Angel Shout'. The Angel Shout was a set of notes that were sung like: 'Lo...lo...lo...' and were sung in descending thirds. The Angel Shout was supposed to call the Shakers to meeting."

"Today I have no reservations about going into the Meeting House, but I will not try my experiment again!" (Pages 34-35, *Shaker Ghost Stories from Pleasant Hill, KY.*)

Shaker Ghost Stories from Pleasant Hill, KY
by Thomas Freese
Published August 2005 by AuthorHouse
ISBN: 1420850725
36 B&W photos, 136 pages
Retail: $13.95

Fog Swirler
and 11 Other Ghost Stories

Illustration by William Church from Fog Swirler

Master storyteller Thomas Freese created twelve tales he calls "fiction that falls not far from fact." A nineteenth century gravedigger discards body parts from the University of Louisville Medical School into a deep well. School children discover a scarecrow filled with cash. The new next door neighbor has the same name, furniture and clothes as the previous man and what is he growing in the greenhouse? A woman discovers a fossilized skeleton and takes him home. Airport workers who get too close to the unclaimed luggage from Salem go missing. What happens to Richard Sears, American businessman who meets a mysterious stranger while both are on vacation in Mexico? Thomas Freese tells twelve short story mysteries, each unique and fascinating. His tales— Ghost Dog, Strawberry Picking, Final Arrangements— weave everyday scenes with bizarre or supernatural surprises.

Excerpt from "Hotbox" with story illustration (above):

It was September, and nearly time for fall baseball. They stopped by Mr. Mitchell's field before school. The weather was still warm, the sun was shining and a scarecrow watched them throw the ball back and forth. They would have rather played hotbox, where two players at two bases practice trying to run down and tag or throw out a runner between them. But as happened before, their runner, Sally Bergman, hadn't been able to join them. The Mitchell farm bordered a small creek and their main goal was keeping the baseball from getting lost in those weeds. On the other side, Mr. Mitchell's cornfield was fallow this year, so the ball could easily be found amongst the year-old stubble of cornstalks.

Luke threw the ball again and again to Sam. Sam was shorter, and Luke sometimes threw it too high for his friend to catch. Sam was a funny guy, one that the boys in their class all enjoyed. He had two older brothers. One was in high school.

Luke caught Sam's hard throw and said, "Gosh you've got the power."

They both laughed, and without really aiming well, Luke threw the baseball high and to Sam's left. It sailed another twenty feet and hit the scarecrow in the stomach, popping open the red flannel shirt.

Sam looked back and said, "Okay Mister, you fix the scarecrow's shirt, and I'll find the ball."

Luke walked over to the scarecrow, chewing his black licorice gum. He was the only kid in fifth grade who chewed that gum. All the girls turned up their noses at the smell and the other boys chewed either Double Bubble or their Dad's tobacco.

Sam had trouble finding the baseball, as it seemed that the ground actually had plenty of baseball colored cornhusks. He used his glove to root around in the husks, not sure if a garden snake might be lying underneath.

"I sure hope you haven't lost this one, Luke Thomas. And we only have another five minutes before we've got to get to school!"

But Luke wasn't really listening. He was standing in front of the scarecrow and his jaw had ceased chewing. He saw that the baseball had split-broken one of the buttons and the shirt was opened by a few inches. But Luke Thomas wasn't prepared to see the hundred dollar bills now sticking out of the shirt.

"Forget about the ball, Sam and get over here now!"

Luke's voice seemed insistent, so Sam walked over to see why Luke was excited. Instantly, Sam saw the money but Luke spoke first. "We'd better leave this here. We should get to school right away. If there's maybe thousands of dollars stuffed in this scarecrow, then someone might be watching us right now!" Both boys glanced at the creek, and at the woods that stood between them and school.

Sam exclaimed, "You've got to fix the shirt before we go!"

"How am I gonna do that? I busted the old shell button." Sam looked at Luke and got a bright idea.

"Use your gum and that'll keep it shut for a while." Luke took his faded black gum out, put the few hundreds sticking out back under the shirt and pressed the gum between shirt sides.

"There, good as new" he said then looking at Sam, "Whatever, you know what I mean."

The boys quickly started walking to school and Sam said, "It must be almost eight, we'd better run."

They both ran through the woods, not having any time to look back and see if anyone was there watching them.

The boys were late and while the secretary wrote tardy slips, they looked at each other silently, each boy wondering who had put the money in the scarecrow. Where did the money come from, and would that someone find out their secret? They weren't able to talk again until lunch, when both boys got permission to take their bag lunches outside and eat.

"You know we left the baseball there," Luke started the conversation.

Sam replied, "It's my ball but I hadn't written my name on it yet." They were both silent for a minute.

"Maybe we shouldn't play hotbox there for a while." Luke quietly suggested.

Sam nodded, his mouth full of turkey sandwich with lettuce. Both boys wondered what it would be like to have that money but neither said anything more...

(Pages 105-107, *Fog Swirler and 11 Other Ghost Stories.*)

Fog Swirler and 11 Other Ghost Stories
by Thomas Freese
Published October 2006 by AuthorHouse
ISBN: 1425950868
5 pen & ink drawings, 129 pages
Retail: $14.95

Ghosts, Spirits and Angels: True Tales from Kentucky and Beyond

Gather around and listen...Thomas Freese tells true tales from friends and folk in Kentucky, Indiana and beyond. Thomas again shows no fear in hunting down the strange, the beautiful, the odd or unexplained. And depending on the character of each spirit manifestation, Thomas categorizes the amazing actions as the visit of a ghost, spirit or angel. Staying late after class one day in graduate school, Thomas heard the story of a friend of a friend coming back from death to provide healing words—Power Tools in Heaven. From the husband of a fellow author, Thomas records the unpleasant details of what is expunged from the soul in healing—Black Spirit Flees Word of God.

The stories from Ghosts, Spirits and Angels come from family, from colleagues, from contacts made at book signings, from chance meetings. Some stories were contributed by our best ghost experts—children, such as God Wears Shiny New Pajamas. Thomas Freese delivers accounts of the scary, the comforting, and the bizarre. His stories include themes familiar to the lovers of ghost stories—haunted homes, animated objects, voices without body, lost objects, mystery figures and loved ones lingering for years!

Ghosts, Spirits and Angels includes over a hundred amazing true stories. A sampling of some of the story titles includes: Old Man on Gravestone, Family Ghost, The Evil Ones Draw Nigh, Help from Beyond the Grave, House Built Over Indian Battleground, Preach or Die, Seeing Back in Time, Ghost Cat, Twice Saved from Death, Flooded Car, Camouflage Angel, White-robed EMT and many more. The tales come from private homes, historic Bed and Breakfast buildings, remote roads, cemeteries, cars, old campgrounds and the highway.

Thomas Freese introduces each teller then allows them to relate the story in their own voice.

Excerpt from *Ghosts, Spirits and Angels*:
"White Horse, Foggy Night" by Lahna Harris, Clarksville, IN.

"Billy" and I met the summer following my graduation from Clarksville High School. The girls from Clarksville seemed to have a fascination with boys from New Albany High School, a neighboring city. My three best friends and I cruised the Ranch House drive-in restaurant in Clarksville for a couple of weeks at the beginning of that summer. Then we decided to cruise Jerry's in New Albany. We liked it as it was more exciting. There were a lot more people there and a *lot* more flirting going on, seemingly non-stop.

One magical night, the four of us were parked next to a car full of boys from New Albany. We saw a few of them before and felt comfortable as we talked back and forth from car to car, joking, laughing. We never saw one of the boys before and it was Billy. He and I didn't seem to see or hear anyone else that night. He got out of the car, walked over by my window and we connected. At age eighteen, it was easy to have an instant crush on him. When my friends and I left Jerry's that night, all I could do was talk about Billy. Pammy, Jan and Holly made fun of me and told me I fell for boys too fast. I hoped I would see him again.

A few nights went by and we didn't see Billy with any of the New Albany boys at Jerry's. Then one night, he showed up, this time apparently driving his own car. He and I spotted each other in the circle of cars that were cruising. He stopped the flow of the merry-go-round movement by getting out of his car, walking over to my car and asking me out. As demure as I had been with advances in the past, I immediately accepted.

By late summer, Billy and I were dating. One night, he drove us on some country roads. I liked driving along dark country roads. He explained that there was a spot to park that was isolated where we wouldn't be bothered, except for one thing that I might not like. He explained that one of his friends had found a place, nestled alongside the back side of a crop field and had a frightening experience. I asked about it and began to feel uneasy. He said he didn't know the details only that his friend said he would never go anywhere near there again.

Billy finally found the spot and pulled in. We were surrounded by what appeared to be hundreds of cornstalks that stretched for miles. It was difficult to see out the car window by this time as it was beginning to get foggy. And it was *soooo* dark. I told Billy I was afraid and he tried to ease my mind. I wanted to go somewhere else. He coaxed me to stay despite my feeling of foreboding.

My mind wandered away from fear for a few moments as Billy kissed me. Suddenly the car was shaken and there was a thumping noise near both back windows and the rear of the car. Billy started the car as fast as he could—wheels spinning in reverse and back out on the country road. It was a blur, both because of the speed in which Billy got us out of there and because of the fog. I saw what appeared to be three figures, though. Neither Billy nor I heard any voices.

I thanked God out loud that we got away from there. Then we began the long, slow, tedious drive through the fog, back to the city. We were both still scared, wondering if whoever was back there would catch up with us. We wouldn't be able to easily see them because the fog was so dense. At one point, we felt confident that we had escaped but then we struggled to stay on the road, to see anything at all in front of us. I helped to navigate by telling Billy if and when I saw either side of the road.

I wondered out loud if Billy had planned the scene in the cornfield as a big practical joke on me. He looked at me in astonishment and asked if I thought he could have faked that kind of fear. That made sense to me. We talked openly about how scared we both still were as we crept along in the oppressive fog. We didn't know if we could make it any farther. It was becoming impossible to see anything at all.

We decided that we would be very lucky if we made it back home that night. My heart was racing with anxiety and I began to pray silently. Then, the most incredible thing happened. Billy stepped on the brakes as we both saw a large, stunningly beautiful white horse appear just yards from the front of the car and in the middle of the road that we could now see.

Billy was so shocked, he uttered some expletives and I just said, "Do you see what I see?" The horse was standing sideways on the road, turned and looked directly at us then disappeared as suddenly as it appeared. We looked at each other in complete disbelief. We confirmed with each other about what we saw and we sighed what seemed to be a hundred sighs of relief. Billy drove on with both us then able to see the road all the way back to town.

Photo and Illustration Credits

Mansion and gate in "The Witch's Rake" taken by Thomas Freese at Edisto Island, South Carolina.

Wood gate in "The Healing Child" taken by Thomas Freese in Robertson County, Kentucky.

Rock arrow on path in "The Healing Child" taken by Thomas Freese at Blackacre State Nature Preserve, Louisville, KY.

River, hills and trees in "Perfect Work Record" taken by Thomas Freese at the Kentucky River Palisades, Jessamine County, KY.

School bus in "Perfect Work Record" taken by Jack Albert in Sonora, KY.

Hand and horned lizard in "Car Rider" taken by Thomas Freese at Bandelier National Monument, New Mexico.

Western highway in "Car Rider" taken by Thomas Freese in Cuyamungue, NM.

Beach scene in "Namphuong" taken by Thomas Freese in Destin, FL.

Clouds and sky in "Strange and Wonderful Thing" taken by Thomas Freese in NM.

Ponderosas and high desert in "Happy Campers" taken by Thomas Freese in Bandelier National Monument.

Closet door in "The Closet" taken by Jack Albert in at the Thurman-Phillips Home in Sonora, KY.

Picture of Thomas Freese taken by Ann Thompson, Louisville, KY.

Center Family Dwelling in "Shaker Ghost Stories" taken by Thomas Freese at Pleasant Hill, KY.

Pen and ink drawing in "Fog Swirler" by William Church, Louisville, KY.

White Horse in *Ghosts, Spirits and Angels* photographed (Byrnes Mill, MO) and art-altered by Jane Freese.

Acknowledgments and Notes

Thanks to Jackie Atchison for editing assistance and to Jean Butler who posed in her Hardin County school bus. Thanks also to Jackie for help with additional photographs and to Jane Freese for the custom image of the White Horse—created from a period photo of our Great Aunts' horse, Dolly. Thanks to Namphuong for her online friendship.

I wrote the dozen stories in roughly the following chronological sequence: The Healing Child, Perfect Work Record, The Witch's Rake, Namphuong, Dust Bunnies, Whispers, Car Rider, Moving Graves, Strange and Wonderful Thing, Ornaments, Happy Campers and The Closet. Two initial titles for this book were "The Healing Child: Stories of Mortal Folly and Moral Grace" and "The Witch's Rake". The Healing Child story was first titled "Sticks and Stones". The stories in the manuscript were written between December 21, 2006 and January 6, 2008. In the final five months of that period I also wrote the majority of *Ghosts, Spirits and Angels*.

It wasn't until I placed the photo for "Happy Campers" in the final manuscript when I noticed the face that appears in the cloud formation.

I enjoy writing both fiction and nonfiction. More and more do I see less and less distinction between the stories rising from my imagination and the true tales I heard from the story contributors. I like creating the narrative but also I find emotional resonance and release in the constructed situations, conflict and relationships in the stories.

As storyteller Mary Hamilton notes, our stories begin with story seeds. The story seed for "Strange and Wonderful Thing" came from the frequent phrase used in the 8th graders' St. Agnes retreat by the facilitator to describe how a group exercise would be "magically" altered. The story seed for Ornaments came with my trimming Jackie's hair near the holidays. Often I visualized a real location or home to better write the descriptive details of place and in "The Closet" I utilized images from the Moreno's Old Louisville home. With The Healing Child I largely pictured my Great Aunts' farm in Jefferson County, Missouri. My writing of Car Rider came from rich visual memories of living 12 years and more visits since 1981 in New Mexico.